T0367386

WINDFALLS

WINDFALLS

SUSAN CONNELLY

iUniverse, Inc.
Bloomington

WINDFALLS

Copyright © 2011 by Susan Connelly.

All rights reserved. No part of this book may be used or reproduced by any means, graphic, electronic, or mechanical, including photocopying, recording, taping or by any information storage retrieval system without the written permission of the publisher except in the case of brief quotations embodied in critical articles and reviews.

Author photo credit: Janice Scammell

iUniverse books may be ordered through booksellers or by contacting:

iUniverse
1663 Liberty Drive
Bloomington, IN 47403
www.iuniverse.com
1-800-Authors (1-800-288-4677)

Because of the dynamic nature of the Internet, any web addresses or links contained in this book may have changed since publication and may no longer be valid. The views expressed in this work are solely those of the author and do not necessarily reflect the views of the publisher, and the publisher hereby disclaims any responsibility for them.

Any people depicted in stock imagery provided by Thinkstock are models, and such images are being used for illustrative purposes only.
Certain stock imagery © Thinkstock.

ISBN: 978-1-4620-4015-5 (sc)
ISBN: 978-1-4620-4016-2 (ebk)

Printed in the United States of America

iUniverse rev. date: 07/23/2011

CONTENTS

Friends——the brightest windfall

ACKNOWLEDGMENTS

Editor, Patty Lane—When it comes to you, my friend, "amazing" works

Writers' groups—Massachusetts and Maine

Readers—For all that you give me

I am not about to say whether this story or that is true.
Herodotus

HALFWAY

*E*lderly housing," Frank's sister is saying. "That's the PC term for it. New digs—same old Sybil."

Frank scowls at the phone as if Marian can see his irritation. It is so typical of her to start up with the negative remarks just when he's decided to visit their grandmother. And he hates the way she says things like "PC" and "digs" to sound young and hip.

"Shoot me first," Marian goes on. "That's what they should call those places."

"Marian—I get the picture. Could you please just give me the directions? I'd like to see her before I go out of town next week."

His sister puts down the phone and goes to look for the directions. She is gone for several minutes.

"Can't find them," she says. "But it's easy." She then lays out a route that is both vague and complicated. Frank stops her when she gets to the Esso station on the left.

"What year are you living in? They haven't had Esso stations since the seventies. Maybe even the sixties."

"Oh, you know what I mean. The one with the red on the sign. Anyway, tell her I said hello."

They hang up, and Frank goes online to locate Cherry Orchard Residences. The website shows a snowy-haired couple dressed in tennis whites, sipping wine in a clubhouse. Ha. Wonder what those dudes made of Sybil.

Dudes. Now he's sounding like Marian. Frank prints the directions and takes them out to his car. The last thing he needs is to be driving in circles looking for an Esso station.

The weather on Saturday is ideal—cool and sunny, with the leaves just beginning to change. Frank wouldn't mind being on the golf course, but he quickly puts that thought aside. Sybil is the last of her generation in his family, and it's not going to kill him to pay her a visit and take her to lunch.

Frank wonders what possessed Sybil to move to Maine, after living her whole life in Worcester, Massachusetts. She was born there, married at sixteen, lived for years in a three-decker with relatives on both the other floors. She's been a widow for thirty years and as far as Frank knows, she doesn't have any friends in Maine. But that's Sybil—she's never felt the need to make any sense.

He stops thinking about his peculiar grandmother and concentrates on the directions. The website said this place wasn't far from the New Hampshire border ("convenient to tax-free shopping"), and Frank has been in Maine for at least twenty minutes. Three traffic lights, then a left and up the hill. Frank sees the sign for Cherry Orchard Residences, across from a gas station. It is a Sunoco.

For once Marian wasn't exaggerating. The place is terrible. Sybil's new home is a ten-story concrete tower covered with corrugated stucco the color of wet beach sand. The parking lot in front of the building is filled with sedans that probably haven't hit 15,000 miles. Old, old people with canes and walkers and wheelchairs creep past at an evolutionary pace. Why move to Maine if you're going to live in a place even more depressing than Worcester?

The lobby is brilliant with fluorescence. Frank examines the name cards and finds Sybil's—S. Green-907. He presses the bell and hears an answering buzz. Several elderly ladies are making their way in from the outside, and Frank holds the inner glass door for what seems like five minutes as they pass through.

The elevator opens on the ninth floor and there is his grandmother, lurking in a doorway just to his left. She beckons him with some urgency and Frank feels his first twinge of annoyance. She's always been weird about her neighbors, sure that they're interested in her comings and goings and who's visiting her. They never have names—just directional codes like Upstairs, or Next Door. Marian once said, in an uncharacteristic flare of wit, that they should plot the latitude and longitude so Sybil could use that.

Seeing that her grandson has gotten the message to hurry, Sybil partially closes the door, leaving him just enough room to enter. He slips through, and the door bumps him as Sybil closes and locks it. They are safe from the neighbors. Frank turns to hug his grandmother, who flaps a hand twice against his lower back to get it over with.

Frank tries not to sigh. He has always wanted a cozy Nana who would call him Frankie and overfeed him. But when God handed out the grandmothers, scrawny, unhuggable Sybil, only forty when he was born, was what he got.

"So this is the place," Sybil says without enthusiasm. Frank dutifully looks around. A tiny kitchenette, a boxy living room, a miniature bedroom and bathroom. His inspection gives him time to get used to Sybil's appearance. She is more wrinkled than he remembered, and there are several gray-green growths on her face that make her look like an extra on Star Trek.

"There's a porch," Sybil says. "We'll look at it later."

Frank wonders how long she expects him to stay, and immediately feels guilty. She's old, for God's sake. What kind of a grandson would have that mean thought about Star Trek? He begins picking out things to admire in the frightful place. The kitchen cabinets have pewter handles. "These are nice," he says.

"Plastic. They come off in your hand."

He begins to feel a little desperate. He fingers one of the half dozen candy dishes scattered about the living room and Sybil says he can have it if he wants. Frank hastily lets go of the dish and says, "So! Where shall we go for lunch?"

Sybil shrugs and walks to the television. She fiddles with the channel selector and a poorly focused gray and white image appears on the screen.

"It's the lobby," she says. "When you rang the buzzer I put the TV on and could tell it was you."

She turns off the set and goes into the bedroom. When she comes back out she is wearing an oversized cotton jacket with lighthouses printed on it. The jacket clashes almost audibly with the cabbage roses on Sybil's blouse, and her pilly yellow pants. As they leave the apartment Sybil says to Frank, "Some of them watch it all day."

"The TV?"

"The lobby."

Frank has visited the pretty parts of Maine, and as they drive to the restaurant he is even more clueless about why Sybil would pick this town. It's very built-up, and every block seems to have a traffic light and special turning lanes. Sybil directs him through several perilous intersections and finally onto a four-lane road. Another mile, and there is the restaurant, huge and designed to resemble a Norman castle.

"They have functions here," Sybil says, yanking ineffectually at her seat belt. Frank reaches over to free her. "I came for somebody's birthday. It was salmon—a lot of them didn't like it."

Several groups are approaching the restaurant, all with at least one enfeebled member. Some are even toting their own oxygen. Frank hopes the place is non-smoking. He tries to give his arm to his grandmother but she steps smartly ahead of him and up the stairs. He wishes she'd act a little more like a sweet old lady being taken to lunch, but he has to admit she looks a lot better than the rest of these ancients, though the full sun does nothing for the growths on her face.

A waitress in a kind of Anne Boleyn get-up shows them to a table in a room as brightly lit as an operating theater. Frank takes his menu and starts to reach into his pocket for his reading glasses. He notices that Sybil is reading the menu without glasses and puts his away. She studies the offerings and asks, "Do you eat haddock? It's OK here."

He looks where she is pointing. The heading on the page reads Senior Specials. For Age 60 and Over. Frank smiles.

"Those are for seniors. I still have a few years to go."

Sybil studies him with her sharp eyes and says carelessly, "They wouldn't say anything."

Frank is stunned by this observation. Is she implying that he could pass for sixty? Or even older? He looks at his hands as if expecting to see liver spots. Before he can ask her to explain herself, Sybil launches a new topic.

"That sister of yours. She's sure one for coming around when she's after money. Or something for those kids." She mimics Marian, rather well, in a falsetto. "*Oh, Sybil, I know I said I wasn't going to ask again, but Jeremy wants those shoes that all his friends are getting . . .*" She drops the Marian voice. "Carol Ann is after my fur coat, but I might give it to Catholic Charities instead."

The waitress appears, and they order. Sybil returns to the subject of Marian. Bored with the steady rant, Frank tries to change the subject.

"While we're talking about family—I always wondered how you got the name Sybil."

She looks at him as if he were monopolizing the conversation.

"It's a name. Now back to Marian."

The food arrives, and is nearly inedible. Frank's salad consists of a pork-white leaf of iceberg lettuce, a strip of stale Bermuda onion, and one cherry tomato. The dressing is not what he ordered. The fettuccini has been cooked to the consistency of Cream of Wheat, and the chicken sits in a puddle of what tastes like fat-free butter substitute. Frank supposes you can't expect *al dente* in a place where most of the customers are *sans* teeth.

"How's the spaghetti?" Sybil asks.

"Good," says Frank. "Fine." He refrains from asking how her lunch is. Will she want dessert? The choices are Jello and ice cream.

Sybil, eating steadily, at last dispenses with the subject of ungrateful Marian and moves on to whether the boy who does Sybil's squash-colored hair is a fruitcake. It takes Frank a minute to realize that his grandmother means that the hairdresser may be gay. Hard upon her musings about the sexual preferences of Mr. Alex, Sybil looks keenly at Frank. "What about you. Got a girl?"

He wishes she'd get *both* the Jello and the ice cream. Anything to shut her up for five minutes. He says, "There's a woman in my office building. We've been to the movies a few times. Once I took care of her son while she went to the dentist."

"A kid and no husband?" Sybil says loudly. "How old?"

"Travis is seven," Frank begins, lowering his voice so she might take the hint and do likewise. Sybil interrupts him.

"The girl. How old?"

Seriously vexed by this rude question, Frank is tempted to make Lisa a buxom twenty-year-old without a wrinkle to her name. But how could she be twenty if Travis is seven? "Forties," he says. "She's divorced."

Sybil snorts. You'd think divorced women were on a par with streetwalkers. Frank opens his mouth to speak but just then the waitress arrives with the check. Frank takes it gratefully, as Sybil begins rummaging in her purse, a straw box with seashells glued to it.

"My treat," Frank says, making one last attempt to play the part of the doting grandson giving his Granny a special outing.

Sybil shakes her head so vehemently that the greenish skin growths wobble.

"We'll each pay for our own," she says. Having learned long ago the uselessness of arguing with her, Frank begins to total the check. "It's twenty dollars with the tip. You had the Senior Special, so yours is less. Why don't you put in five, and I'll put in fifteen?"

Sybil hands him a five and three ones. "I went to school. It was a long time ago, but I can still add."

Frank takes the money, realizing that her math is exactly correct. Sybil gathers the lighthouse jacket around her and they leave the now-crowded restaurant. Frank's car is one of the few in the parking lot without Handicapped plates.

On the drive back Sybil asks when he'll be leaving. He glances at his dashboard clock—two-ten—and says, "I should be on the road by three. The traffic . . ."

"We'll sit on my porch. I've got ice cream."

They pull into the visitor lot and walk into a lobby filled with people complaining about the slowness of the elevator. The women all stare or smile at Frank, but Sybil makes no introductions. She points to a posted notice of the day's activities.

"That's today. Mass at one-thirty. Blood pressure check at four."

As Sybil is unlocking her door an elderly man creeps exaggeratedly up behind her and squeezes her waist. Frank expects an explosion—Sybil hates to be touched—but she seems delighted, beaming and slapping flirtatiously at the skinny man, who wears a red and blue plaid shirt and tan pants printed with suitcases.

"This," says Sybil in Frank's direction, "is my neighbor. Rupert the pest." She does not say who Frank is. The three of them stand in the doorway while Sybil and Rupert complain animatedly about the morning's testing of the smoke detectors. Apparently the residents were not properly notified.

"It's just a dirty trick to get into your apartment," Sybil says, and Rupert nods authoritatively. She addresses her next remark to Frank

"They hate it when they don't find you until you've been dead for a couple of days."

Sybil spares Frank the necessity of responding to this by pushing open the door and waving him inside, leaving the garishly-outfitted Rupert standing in the hall.

"He really *is* a pest." Sybil says. "If he knew we were having ice cream we'd never get rid of him."

They sit on her coffin-shaped porch in straight kitchen chairs and eat butter pecan ice cream. Frank hates butter pecan, but he keeps quiet, knowing his deliverance is at hand. Sybil, who has given no indication of having enjoyed Frank's visit, begins to talk about "the next time you come." She even speaks of returning the visit, and asks if there is bus service between this down-at-the-heels place and the wealthy suburb where Frank lives. He is touched by her naiveté and pats her shoulder.

"We'll figure something out," he says. "I'd like you to see my place." He knows it will never happen.

Sybil holds still for a two-second hug and tells Frank she will wave to him from the window. He makes sure to roll down the car window so she can't miss seeing his arm flapping cheerfully as he contemplates his grandmother in the rear-view mirror.

Once he's on the road, Frank takes out his cell phone and speed dials Lisa's number. She's a computer programmer and goes to work at four—he should be able to just catch her before she leaves for the office. He wishes he had thought to tell Sybil about Lisa's job. She probably pictured an over-the-hill waitress in hot pants.

Travis answers the phone. "Hey, big guy," Frank says self-consciously, and then has to listen to Travis describe in detail some violent computer game he's been playing. Frank winces as the boy screams in his ear ". . . and he DIES!" and ". . . POW–he's blown away!" It's after 3:30, and Frank cuts in. "Sounds great, Trav. Get your Mom, OK?"

"Ma!" Travis yells, and drops the phone. In a moment Lisa comes on, sounding harried.

"Frank? Do you hear that racket? Travis was supposed to bring home *one* kid, but there was some mix-up. Supposedly."

She talks on, as self-centered as Sybil, until Frank breaks in the same way he did with Travis. "I saw my grandmother."

"Oh, right." Lisa doesn't sound very interested. "How is she?"

"Good, I guess. I mean, she's ninety. I hope I'm doing that good in another forty years."

There is a crash, and screams. Lisa shouts at the boys then says into the phone, "My God, is that the time? I've got to go."

"Right," Frank says. "I'll call you when you get to work." He watches a tour bus pass him in the center lane. "Lee . . ."

"What, Frank?" He knows she is looking at the kitchen clock.

"Do you ever think of me as old?"

There is silence, and he thinks she has hung up. Then she says, "Frank, I'm late. And to tell you the truth, I'm not in the mood for that subject right now. Call me later, and we'll talk about something more cheerful."

"But you didn't . . ." he says, and hears her hang up. He stares at the phone. Couldn't she have just said no?

The big bridge that connects Maine and New Hampshire is in sight. Since Lisa was no help, Frank is convincing himself. "Fifty is nothing these days," he says. "Even *sixty* is nothing." His tires bump and catch, and he is on the bridge. Frank looks straight ahead and sees a sight to behold.

The fine October weather has decided to stay in Maine. Halfway across the bridge, just where the arc of green steel begins to descend, the sky is dark and rain is pouring down. A half century lived, and here is a first.

EULOGY

$\mathscr{F}$rom the expressway, Frank can see the three-deckers and churches that to him typify the city of his birth. The neighborhood where his grandmother Sibyl lived for most of her ninety-four years looked very like the ones he is passing—but then, most of the neighborhoods do. The last of her generation, Sibyl is being buried tomorrow in the vast Catholic cemetery where she served as unofficial tender of countless potted geraniums.

His MapQuest directions, the print enlarged for Frank's middle-aged eyes, guide him to an exit ramp, left and left again, to a chain motel across from a mall. Pedestrians are taking their lives in their hands walking along the shoulder of the four-lane highway, piled with blackened March snow. Frank had intended to stay downtown, but the Special Olympics had filled all the hotels near the convention center, which is how he finds himself pulling into a half-plowed parking lot with a sign disclaiming any liability for stolen guest vehicles.

The man at the desk—Rafael, reads his plastic name tag—is talking in Spanish with a man leaning against a linens cart. Frank waits, the hook on his garment bag digging into his hand. Overhead, a Spanish soap opera plays on the television.

"Mañana," the man with the cart says to the clerk, and turns to smile at Frank. This gesture of acknowledgment, a human welcome, stirs something in Frank. He realizes that, although he is only a few miles from Sibyl's old tenement, he will never see her again. Except, of course, in the good old Catholic tradition as a rouged corpse.

Rafael can't seem to find Frank's reservation. After ten minutes of watching the clerk make futile mouse clicks, Frank goes back out to his car to get the confirmation number. He takes the opportunity to move the Lexus under a floodlight, wishing he hadn't stopped as he entered the city for a deluxe car wash, or declined the rental company's optional insurance. With both ex-wives after him for back alimony and the IRS on his case, Frank couldn't buy the leather dashboard on this car, but he's determined to keep up appearances. Sibyl's friends assured him constantly of the pride she took in her grandson's success.

The confirmation number does the trick—Frank receives an apology for the inconvenience and an envelope advertising breakfast pastries and containing two key cards. Once inside the small room he hangs up his suit bag, noticing with distaste that the floor of the closet contains a candy wrapper and a sock. He's meeting his sister Marian and the priest at seven for dinner—it's only four now. Frank reaches for his coat, thinking that even the mall is sure to be an improvement over three hours in this cramped space.

When he gets there, though, the mall is not much more appealing than his motel room. Tiled expanses, Radio Shack, chain clothing stores, a food court. The Waldenbooks he saw listed on the directory is steel-gated, with empty shelves. Frank walks the length of the mall, to Sears, where a teenage couple are having a dolled-up baby's photo taken with the Easter Bunny. The baby's wide brown eyes stare at the giant rabbit, whose smile is part of its whiskered mask. The young father, who is unsmiling, wears baggy shorts and a cap turned backwards.

Frank kills an hour at the mall, looking at cookware and windup flashlights, then makes his way down the slippery access road to the highway. The pedestrian light appears to be broken, so he waits for a break in the traffic, then sprints across the road. He reaches the other side safely, only to be nearly hit by an SUV peeling out of a Dunkin Donuts drive-through. Shaken, he plods through the trampled snow back to the motel, wondering how Marian might have coped if she had to bury brother and grandmother on the same day.

He sees the message light flashing as he enters the room. Marian—who else could it be? His sister's long message is disconnected and weepy. She and Sibyl complained constantly about each other, but now that Sibyl has "passed," Marian is a bundle of grief-stricken nerves. Her message concerns funeral details—flowers, music—which he has repeatedly told her are up to her. He calls her back, calms her down, and promises not to be late for the restaurant.

In fact, he is early, but Marian and the priest are already there, seated at a booth, watching the entrance for him. They both stand as Frank approaches the booth, and Marian leans over to kiss him.

"Frank, this is Father Dave. Father, this is my brother."

The men shake hands. Father Dave is tall and robust-looking, with curly graying hair. Frank wonders if the celibate life accounts for the youthful appearance of some of the priests he has known. Sibyl talked about this one all the time, proud to be on a quasi-first name basis with a man of the cloth.

"Is this place all right?" Marian asks. "I thought we should pick some place out of the way, so it's not full of all those retarded kids."

Oh, Christ. Frank says, "Marian . . ." but before he can say anything further Father Dave smiles broadly and says, "It's just fine with me as long as the menu isn't all steak."

"You don't like steak? Frank and I wanted to treat you to a nice big sirloin."

The priest looks abashed. "That's very nice of you. I like it fine. It's just that—well, I'm a priest, and it's a Friday during Lent."

Marian opens her mouth, then closes it. She squeezes her eyes shut.

"I cannot possibly believe I did this."

"It's not a problem," Father Dave says. "I'm sure . . ."

"Do you even begin to understand," Marian laments, "how Sibyl would kill me if she found out about this?"

Considering such a beginning, dinner goes pretty well. The menu has lobster as well as several cuts of steak, so that problem is solved. (Although Frank, who knows the bill will end up on his strained MasterCard, wonders apprehensively what "market price" will turn out to be.) Marian has two glasses of wine in rapid succession and begins to speak sentimentally of her grandmother. Frank would love a martini—it was a long drive, with several traffic tie-ups—but he feels that somebody should keep the priest company in his abstinence. He is relieved to see the food arriving before Marian can get it into her head that a third drink would hit the spot.

Father Dave talks entertainingly of Sibyl—her humor, sociability, wry opinions. The person he is describing bears no resemblance to the secretive, bossy woman Frank knew his whole life. Was there some way he could have known this other Sibyl, if she actually existed?

In the restaurant parking lot, the three stand by Marian's car, a scarlet convertible that Frank privately thinks is inappropriate for a woman in her fifties, and agree to meet at the funeral home the following morning. Frank drives back to the motel and turns on the television as soon as he's in his room. He changes out of his suit while watching the program schedule, and sees that the Oscars are on. Sibyl, who hadn't been to the movies in decades, loved that overlong, hyped show. She said she liked to see what people were wearing. Frank uses the remote to find the program, just as if he and Sibyl were going to be on the phone the next day debating whether Renee Zellweger's train was really a bit much.

He sleeps poorly—the Oscars ran late, and the room is stuffy. His telephone wake-up call jolts him from an exhausted comatose state. After showering and dressing in the dark suit, he goes to find the Complimentary Breakfast Room advertised on his key card holder. Scruffily dressed people sit spaced out as far as possible from one another, spooning cereal and reading *USA Today*. Frank carries a bagel and paper cup of coffee back to his room and eats while watching television replays of the Oscar speeches.

Marian has been quite definite that the family is to meet at the funeral home an hour before the service. She is waiting there with her son and daughter, neither of whom Frank has seen in years. Carol Ann nods at Frank, then talks exclusively to her mother, while Jeremy slouches to the other side of the room and leans against the flocked wallpaper, text-messaging on his cell phone. Both kids are dressed as if for a day on the ski slopes.

Soft-spoken men in black suits come and go, consulting with Marian about final details of the service. At quarter of ten Frank's sister takes a mirror from her purse and examines her face, then says to Frank, "Do you want to do the eulogy?"

He can't have heard her correctly. "On ten minutes notice you're asking me if I want to do the eulogy?"

"You don't have to get like that. I just thought of it."

"Marian, a eulogy is the sort of thing you *prepare*. People expect certain things. You don't just get up there like a kid with a book report."

"Well, it's not like I know what to say. I suppose I could thank her for the money, but no way would she want these biddies knowing about that."

"That's not the sort of . . ." What she has just said belatedly registers. "Marian, what money?"

She flushes, looks down, folds the mirror. "I was going to tell you afterwards."

"*What money.*"

"Sibyl's. She left it to me."

The funeral home is appropriately hushed, but now a sensation of deafness fills Frank's ears. Marian is saying something, but it's as if he's wearing earplugs.

"Frank?"

He can hear. Now to try his voice.

"Marian, are you telling me that Sibyl left you everything?"

Their grandmother had lived frugally, even stingily. In recent years Frank helped with her finances and tax returns. There had been real estate, and well-chosen stocks. Sibyl died rich.

Marian is now twisting a wad of pink tissue. "She said you didn't need any money."

Out of the corner of his eye Frank sees two of the funeral home employees watching them nervously. He breathes deeply several times, like a man who has nearly drowned. He *didn't need any money.*

One of the black-suited men starts toward him, and Frank manufactures a smile that appears to reassure the guy. The smile is still pasted on his face when he turns back to Marian.

"I'll do it."

"Do what?"

"The eulogy."

As family, Frank and Marian are in the front row, with her kids next to her. Carol Ann is looking around constantly like an arrested toddler, and Jeremy still has his phone out. When Father Dave comes out in his vestments the kid only holds the phone out of sight while continuing to stare at its miniature screen.

The Mass is a farce. None of Sibyl's family has a clue about the responses, and because they're in the front row they can't look for direction to those in the know. Frank suddenly realizes that his name has been spoken—twice.

". . . grandson Francis will deliver the eulogy."

Frank stands, and after a startled moment Marian steps into the aisle to let him out of the pew. He follows a patterned runner to the altar steps and climbs them to the podium, where he adjusts the microphone. The church is about half full—dozens of wizened faces turn up to him.

"My grandmother was a unique individual."

This gets several smiles and titters. He has started off on the right note.

"She wouldn't appreciate it one bit if I mentioned her age . . ." (More chuckles) "but in her—why don't we call it a full life—she definitely had her personality quirks."

Like a skilled showman he has caught their interest. They are along for the ride. Frank tells a humorous but appropriate anecdote (God knows what Marian would have come up with) about taking Sibyl to buy a winter coat, and another about his grandmother's love-hate relationship with her Buick. He looks discreetly at his watch—coming up on seven minutes. He doesn't want to be like those assistant directors at the Oscars who won't get off the stage.

His gaze moves over the attentive faces. They're all waiting for him to deliver the final word on Sibyl. Well, here it comes.

Frank draws in a breath so that what he is about to say will come out exactly right. And as he does so, he hears a voice inside his head. Not Sibyl or God or even his conscience. It is his own voice.

Be the first ever in this family. Have some class.

He waits for several seconds, during which a few people move restlessly. He knows what he is going to do, and also knows that he will not regret it. Smiling, he lifts his hands from the podium, a secular benediction. He sees and hears that the fidgeting has ceased.

"I knew my grandmother my whole life. Again, we'll omit mention of exactly how long that was."

Is it his imagination, or do the titters sound relieved? Did his hearers suspect how close he had come? Frank leans slightly forward over the podium and offers what is expected—a loving grandson's rueful wisdom.

"But now that she's gone, I realize that I didn't really know her until the very end. And because of that, I have a piece of advice for every one of you."

Sibyl's friends are returning Frank's smile. He looks from face to face.

"Don't make the same mistake I did. Thank you."

ETTA

*I*n the year 1932, in a town in the low mountains of western Massachusetts, a woman named Etta Grimes plucked a baby from his carriage as easily as one might pluck a low-hanging apple.

What would impel a woman who would never think of stealing an apple to steal a baby? And then to be resolute in thinking she had done nothing wrong? Almost everybody who was there is gone—this is the story they told among themselves, and later to their children.

It was the third year of the Depression, and Etta was forty-eight years old. She looked quite a bit older, in the way of eccentric people who live alone with no one to keep an eye on their dress and mannerisms. Etta had not always lived alone. Until the beginning of 1930 she had lived with her mother, a demanding woman whose hypochondria had been her undoing when no one believed she really *was* ill this time. Etta had barely buried her mother when the local bank failed, and her small savings disappeared along with those of most of her neighbors.

At first, Etta managed. She got work cleaning houses, and was a familiar sight around town with her chopped, graying hair and dresses altered from her mother's stout size. People would wave and smile and call, "Hello there, Etta," and she would always wave back, seldom speaking or calling anyone by name. She was a regular at church, arriving always just as the service began and hurrying out with a shy nod to the minister moments after the last hymn.

Then the summer came, and the town had its second close look at the reality of life after Black Friday. The wealthy people who owned vacation homes in the town did not return to them, or send their children back to the summer camps along the cold, clean river. The caretakers who kept the grass cut and the flowers tended still had work here and there, but there was nothing for the house painters and delivery men, and there was nothing for Etta. The windows she had polished were curtained that summer, the furniture behind them covered in sheets.

Still, Etta and her neighbors had a better time of it than the jobless in the cities all over America. The town was small enough so that people with very little helped out those with even less. Etta had always tended a vegetable garden for her mother, who would not eat anything that came out of a can, and the crop that year of potatoes and butter beans and stringy carrots kept Etta going. She had chickens and a cow and was strong enough to do most of the yard work herself, with occasional help from a neighboring boy or girl sent to Etta's place with orders to say, Yes, please, to the offer of lemonade, and No, thank you, to the offer of a nickel.

Even afterward, no one could claim to have noticed a real change in Etta. The town had more than its share of quirky personalities, and was even a little proud of them. Etta continued to go to church and keep herself neat, and she still managed to pay for candles and other necessities that her own hard work could not produce. In the end, it may have been a small luxury that brought about the inexplicable thing she did. It may have been the picture show—the first and only such event in Etta's quiet life.

The city where the picture show was playing was less than forty miles from Etta's home, but she had never visited there. Her mother thought that cities were places of vice, from which a young woman would not return with her virtue intact. Of course she didn't put it so to her daughter, but said only, "There's nothing there for us." In time Etta grew uneasy about the very idea of being away from home, and lost any desire she might have had to experience the world. Then, in July, a letter came from the county probate court, and the rhythm of Etta's life was broken.

The letter was delivered on a Saturday morning, by Charles Grant, who had held the position of the town's postmaster for about a decade. He was a decent fellow, a bit pompous about his role as a government agent, and would not answer to 'Charlie'. It made no difference in Etta's case, for she would not have dreamed of calling him anything other than 'Mr. Grant'.

"Well, Etta," he said, coming up the lane to where his customer was tending tomato vines in the front yard. "What you been up to? Looks like you got the court writing to you."

Etta stood, wiping her hands on the front of a gray apron that had belonged to her mother. She made no move to take the letter, and after a moment Charles Grant held it out to her.

"Might as well see what they want," he said, and waited. If Etta thought his interest in her affairs at all strange she did nothing to show it. She took the letter from him and said in the slow way of country people, "I guess there's lemonade for you, Mr. Grant."

This was ample show of hospitality for Charles Grant to follow her inside the small house, where she got lemonade out of the icebox, and sliced one of her fresh tomatoes for the postman. She then cleaned the knife carefully and asked whether Mr. Grant would like salt for his tomato. Knowing that salt was in short supply, he replied that the tomato was fine just the way it was. Etta gave everything a last wipe, dried her hands on a towel, and at long last slit open the envelope.

"I thought I was going to have to wait for the Last Trumpet," Charles Grant would tell his friends that evening in the diner where, as a bachelor, he customarily had his supper. "I thought she was never going to get around to opening that letter."

According to Charles Grant, Etta also took her time about reading the letter once she had taken it from the envelope. She appeared to read it twice, then spoke to the postmaster with her eyes still on the paper in her hand.

"I have to go there," she said, and before Charles Grant could reply she did at last look up at him. Her expression was bewildered, and her eyes were full of fear.

That night, when Charles Grant had finished his story about Etta's letter, there were a number of suggestions as to what should be done. Following the postmaster's lead, no one gave a moment's thought to whether the matter might be private. Etta was thought to be a bit simple, and it was the responsibility of her neighbors to make sure she didn't ignore the letter, which had after all come from the county court.

"I tell you what," said Charles Grant, after everyone else had had a chance to speak his mind. Charles considered himself to be in charge of this impromptu committee, since he had delivered the letter. "Why don't I stop by Ethan's? He'd be the one to handle this."

Ethan Rich was the sheriff, a well-liked man in his mid forties, with a wife and four children. Charles Grant and the sheriff sat at the Riches' kitchen table drinking coffee while Charles told his story. By the time Charles got up to leave, calling his thanks to the sheriff's wife for the good coffee, an agreement had been reached that Ethan would drive out to see Etta on the following day.

The contents of the letter turned out to be a simple matter. Etta's mother's will was about to be probated. In order for Etta to gain legal title to the house in which she had always lived, she would need to appear before a judge and present the papers she had received, signed and notarized.

The sheriff thought Etta would be relieved by his explanation and assurance that she was not in any trouble. But she seemed distraught, on the verge of tears. "I can't," she said, and began twisting at her apron. "It's too far!"

The sheriff began to feel a little exasperated by Etta's failure to grasp the situation, but then quickly realized she must be worried about how she would make the trip. He spoke to her in the same patient voice he used with his five-year-old Margaret, who was sensitive and quick to cry.

"Doris and I will take you, Etta," he said. "She has a sister up that way. We'll just drop her off and then you and I will go to this hearing."

As soon as the word "hearing" was out of his mouth, Ethan Rich realized he hadn't made the most reassuring choice of words. Quickly the sheriff added, "Nothing to it. You'll be on your way in five minutes. And as for me, why I'd say this is official business."

So it was decided, and on a humid morning three weeks later the sheriff, with his wife beside him in their tan Ford, drove to Etta's house to pick her up. Etta was waiting on the front porch. She had on her church dress and hat, and was holding a straw purse that contained the court papers. Doris Rich asked Etta whether she would like to sit up front, but Etta said no and fell into a silence that lasted for the entire trip. This was not a problem, since the sheriff's wife was a great talker and never had need of a response before going on to her next topic.

The sheriff was quite correct that the probate hearing was a simple process, but Etta would probably have had trouble if he hadn't been there. Throughout the brief proceeding she turned to Ethan Rich for help in answering the few questions put to her, and her relief was apparent when Ethan gave her a firm nod to let her know it was over. As the judge signed the papers he took unofficial note of the address of Etta's property.

"Good fishing up that way," he said. Etta looked anxiously toward Ethan Rich, who winked to let her know that nothing was required of her.

"Best there is," he responded, to the judge.

By the time Etta and the sheriff arrived to pick up the sheriff's wife it was lunchtime, and Doris's sister insisted they all stay for the fried chicken and potato salad that was waiting under a damp towel in the icebox. The food was very good, and after a brisk round of compliments to the cook, the guests set to cleaning their plates in anticipation of the cinnamon-blueberry coffee cake, which had won their hostess more than one blue ribbon. It was over the cake and coffee (Etta shyly admitted when asked that she would prefer milk), that Doris Rich brought up the subject of the picture show.

"Ethan," she began, addressing her husband as if it were just the two of them, "Daisy's been telling me about this fine picture that's playing at the Rialto. It's all about a sharpie lawyer and gangsters and such. Do you think . . . could you and me and Etta take ourselves to the matinee?"

Ethan Rich was very fond of his wife and well aware that her vivacious nature must sometimes yearn for treats not readily available to a country mother of four. He quickly agreed to the proposal, remarking that if there were bad guys in the picture he could probably get a few tips on how to handle them. It was not nearly as easy to convince Etta, who had certainly never been to the movies and had no doubt been warned by her mother about their sinfulness. She was quite adamant, and the sheriff was just about to tell his wife not to press the matter further when Etta abruptly had a change of heart.

"You've been most kind," she said, "and I ought to have better manners. I'd be pleased to see this picture show." Her hands pressed against her purse, which had remained in her lap throughout lunch, and she said with unusual firmness, "I'll treat."

Doris Rich started to speak and was silenced by a look from her husband. Etta's pride was at stake. The Riches agreed, with thanks, to her paying for the tickets, and there was a brisk round of goodbyes and thank yous and polite refusals of the leftover chicken, until at last the Riches and Etta were in the car and on their way back to the center of town.

In those days, movie houses were the height of elegance, in keeping with the bright dreams flickering on the screen. The Riches tried to appear at home in the red and gold opulence, but Etta made no such pretense. She stared around her in complete awe, and when the piano started up and the velvet curtains opened, she seemed to struggle to take her eyes from the stunning decor and fix them on the screen.

The main feature was preceded by a portentous newsreel and then a short, innocently suggestive film in which diapered toddlers, including the ringleted Shirley Temple, flirted and intrigued in a milk bar. Doris Rich sighed a few times with apparent pleasure over the antics of this Hollywood version of babies, but Etta and Ethan were silent, perhaps waiting for the gangster picture to begin. Once it did, it proved to be filled with satisfying melodrama. In addition to the "sharpie lawyer," who became a drunkard after an innocent man was executed, the plot included a pugilist, a vial of poison, embezzled funds, and a chaste office-girl. The small matinee audience applauded enthusiastically as the picture ended and the lights came up, causing everyone to blink in the sudden brightness.

The sheriff shepherded his companions up the carpeted aisle and out through the lobby into the daylight. Doris was already talking about the picture, especially about the honorable little typist, whom Doris was much taken with. Ethan Rich had had years of practice at being able to anticipate the precise moment at which his wife would need to pause for breath, and when this finally happened he took the opportunity to speak to Etta.

"Well, Etta," he said, "Doris and I do thank you for that treat. How did you like the show?"

For a moment, Etta did not seem to have heard him, and it seemed that Doris was about to speak again. But just then Etta gave the sheriff and his wife a most uncharacteristic look, free of shyness, rapturous and almost young.

"Oh, my," she said, "Mr. and Miz Rich—did you see that child dance?"

Upon the travelers' return home, Ethan gave informal interviews to his townspeople about Etta's court appearance and assured everyone that the legal matter was "all taken care of." Once people grasped that the court proceeding had been completely without drama and involved no inheritance money, they moved on to questions about Doris's sister (who had been a local girl), and the movie. Doris was in her element, repeating the plot for weeks, and relating key scenes whenever possible to her own life. ("I had a sweet little hat like that myself," she was heard to say. "That is until I was carrying Robert into church and he took a good chomp out of it. He was teething, you know . . .")

Etta had little to say about the trip, other than that she had liked it fine. She volunteered no details about what must have been a total departure from her normal routine, and after a few days Charles Grant summed up the consensus of Etta's neighbors by shaking his head and saying with a grin, "She's a funny one."

Still, Etta seemed a little more sociable after the trip. She would actually exchange greetings with the families she saw at church and once conversed for several minutes with the Riches' bashful Margaret about the child's new white shoes and matching purse. When the Russells had their twins christened, Etta came early to church and sat just a few rows behind the family, beaming at the babies in their lace gowns. Doris Rich went so far as to say it was a pity there had never been a nice fellow for Etta.

The day Etta took the baby was the first warm, sunny day after two days of needed rain. The story of what happened was put together in bits and pieces, since only Etta could have told it all, and she proved unable to do so. The baby was four months old and belonged to a young couple who had recently moved to town after a great-uncle left them his house. The couple also had a daughter, who was four and less than thrilled to have a new baby taking up her mother's time and attention. The mother, well aware of young Jane's feelings, was keeping a close watch that day on both the older child, who was playing with a doll in the front yard, and the baby, asleep in his carriage.

The sun had brought out insects, and when the mother saw a bee hovering near the carriage, she moved quickly to check the mesh covering. Jane watched her mother lift the netting, then put her face down to the baby and make a cooing sound.

"Mommy!" Jane called. "Watch me! Watch what I can do."

She then attempted a cartwheel in the wet grass. Her foot slipped, and she landed clumsily, opening a small cut on her knee. Jane clutched at her tiny wound and raised an uproar.

"Oh, Jane," the mother said, hurrying to her daughter. "Let me see. That little thing? Now stop all that noise and we'll clean it off."

Mother and daughter went inside, with Jane limping dramatically. They were gone just long enough for Jane's mother to dab the cut with a wet cloth and apply a Bandaid, before hurrying back outside to look in the carriage. The baby was gone.

She lifted the blanket and shook it, then gave the carriage a jounce as if to bounce the baby into view. She looked around her as if the baby might have gotten out and be just nearby. Then, in total panic, she ran next door. The neighbor's first thought was that a wild animal had snatched the baby. Kidnappings might happen to wealthy celebrities like the Lindberghs, but not to people in little towns where any stranger would be quickly noticed. The neighbor had a phone, and in no time at all the town operator had cleared the party line and Ethan Rich was on his way.

When Ethan arrived in his sheriff's car his wife was with him. It had taken the Riches only a moment to decide that anything involving a baby might require a woman's presence, and a neighbor of the Riches had been quickly enlisted to watch for the school bus that would bring the Rich children home. Doris was out of the car and onto the porch before her husband had set the parking brake.

After that, things happened quickly. Other neighbors, seeing the sheriff's car, gathered on the sidewalk and Ethan asked the group whether anyone had seen anything. While her husband was trying to get people to speak one at a time, Doris's attention was caught by a curtain moving across the street. Gert Toomey, a widow in her eighties kept mostly housebound by arthritis, was waving to her.

Everybody's attention was focused on the mother, sobbing out her story, so Doris quietly crossed the street and let herself in Gert's front door. "Gert," she said, without any of the usual socializing, "Did you see somebody come by and take Marcie's baby?"

"That I did," Gert began. "She stopped to look and was smiling and smiling at him, then she just lifted him out and walked off."

"Who!" Doris saw that Gert looked startled, and hurt. "Gert, I'm sorry—it's just that we need to get this straightened out right away. Who did you see?"

"Etta," Gert said. Doris could tell Gert was upset with her for raising her voice. "Who else would do a thing like that?"

Without even closing Gert Toomey's door, Doris hurried back to the growing crowd in the Lansings' yard and got her husband's attention. She whispered in his ear, and Ethan's eyes widened, then he took his wife's arm and steered her toward their car, calling back to the others, "Everything's fine! Everybody just wait right here!"

During the short drive to Etta's house Doris Rich was completely silent. What had happened was beyond her understanding, and she must have had uppermost in her mind the hope that the baby was safe. As Ethan pulled the car to a stop Doris finally spoke.

"Dear," she said, "I should go in first."

Ethan looked at her for a moment, then nodded. Doris got out of the car and walked past the flower garden to the door. She knocked twice and called. There was no answer, and Doris pushed open the unlocked door and stepped inside.

Etta was in the parlor, in the rocking chair that had been her Daddy's. She had the baby in her arms and was singing to him as the chair clicked back and forth. The tune had no words, just a low sweetness, a woman's song to a baby. The baby himself was sound asleep.

"Etta?" Doris said, whispering like a person in church. Behind her she heard Ethan enter the house and she waved a hand to let him know that he should not speak. "Etta," she said again, "it's Miz Rich."

Etta made no response. She seemed not to hear. Doris moved to the rocker and rested a hand on Etta's shoulder.

"Etta," she said, "you've taken fine care of this little fellow. But he has to go back to his Mama now."

Under Doris's hand Etta's shoulders dropped, although she still did not speak. She turned to look at Doris, who would remember for the rest of her life the look in Etta's eyes. When in later years she would speak of the incident Doris would wipe her own eyes and say, "I just never did see a woman look so *hungry*." The two women stared at one another, then Etta rocked back once and let her arms go slack so Doris could take the baby.

Perhaps things would have been different if Etta had been willing or able to give any kind of explanation of her actions. The baby's parents, though upset and angry, were not vindictive people, but it was not enough for them to hear other people's theories about what had been going through Etta's head when she lifted the little boy from his carriage. Etta herself did not help her case when, being pressed to say why she had taken the baby, she replied stubbornly and without contrition, "Seems like a woman ought to have a young one." In the end, the court decided that the best thing would be for Etta to spend some time in the county hospital, overseen in those days by the State Board of Health, Lunacy and Charities.

Etta never came home. She did not seem to mind being at the hospital, and for quite a while received frequent visits from her old neighbors. Doris Rich went faithfully every Sunday, and would sit next to Etta and tell her all the news, while Etta rocked and sometimes hummed, the same wordless tune she had sung to the baby. Doris made sure nobody let Etta find out that, after years of heartrending controversy, their town was taken by eminent domain for the building of a reservoir, Etta's home and those of her neighbors drowned beneath the man-made flood. She died in the hospital in 1939, two weeks before Hitler invaded Poland.

The baby is seventy now, a quiet, contented man with a large family. He lives a long way from the lost town in which he was once part of Etta's story. On summer evenings, he sits out in his small yard as the night grows cool. Sometimes a breeze will carry a thread of a tune to him and he closes his eyes to try to hold it, but always it is soon gone.

MOLLY ALONE

*S*now began falling just at dusk on President's Day, large wet flakes that burst against the fogged car windshield and made the driving slippery. Joanna worked the defroster controls back and forth without much effect and felt grateful for the unusually light traffic. She supposed a lot of people were spending school vacation week at Disney or some other warm place, or just snug at home. Joanna was on her way to the hospital to visit her sister. On the car seat beside her was a tissue-wrapped package containing a purple stuffed pig—a fortieth birthday present for Molly.

Joanna passed the brightly lit entrance for Emergency and turned into Visitor Parking, signaling even though there was no one behind her. Usually, visiting friends in this hospital, she had to cruise around looking for a space, but tonight there were several just a few rows from the main entrance. The snow had covered the parking lot lines, and Joanna pulled into what she hoped was only one space. With the engine off, an instant chill filled the car. She drew her coat around her and hurried toward the glass doors of the hospital.

The hospital, like the roads, seemed almost deserted. An elderly volunteer with short bluish curls and a pink smock looked up as Joanna approached the circular information desk. "Good evening. May I help you?"

"I'm here to see Molly Peters," Joanna said. "I got a call that she was admitted this afternoon."

"Peters," said the woman, inexpertly maneuvering the computer mouse. "Not Arthur Peters . . . Would it be Mary?"

"Yes," Joanna said. "Mary Peters. We call her Molly." It wasn't nearly as simple as that, but this stranger matching patient with visitor didn't need to hear the story of Molly's name.

"She's on . . . three," the volunteer said, and frowned. She looked at Joanna a little defensively. "It says Room 308. The thing is, they usually don't put patients on three. It's labs and storage . . ."

"I'm sure it's right," Joanna said, and was halfway to the elevators when it occurred to her that she should have apologized for her abrupt tone.

Joanna had been four when Molly was born. There was already a plump, cute little brother, Danny, and Joanna had amused her elders by insisting on a baby sister this time. At four she was a strong-minded little girl with hazel eyes that would fix sternly on her listener as she made her position clear. No one was surprised when the call came to Grandma's house that Joanna had gotten her wish.

Molly seemed fine at first. She was one of those all-smiles babies that everyone wants to hug and kiss—even people who aren't all that crazy about babies. Her eyes were the same hazel as Joanna's, and she had a wisp of straight brown hair that Joanna liked to tie into a topknot as Molly lay contentedly in her playpen. "There," Joanna would say. "Now I'll sing."

The song was *Molly Malone*, which Joanna had learned from a record of Irish Favorites.

In Dublin's fair city
Where girls are so pretty,
I first set my eyes on sweet Molly Alone . . .

Joanna's mistake was an understandable one. She knew that "Molly" was a name, but "Malone" meant nothing to her, so she picked the closest word she did know. She'd heard the word "alone" often enough when her mother, hearing her teasing Danny, would say, "Leave your brother alone."

Her parents encouraged Joanna to sing the Molly Alone song whenever there were guests. Some of these, after clapping, would give Joanna money for her piggy bank—further proof that Joanna had been right to specify a sister.

As can be the case with first-born children, Joanna was good at amusing herself quietly around grownups, and it was easy to forget she was nearby. Joanna would be coloring or looking at books in the room she now shared with Molly, and gradually the low voices of her grandmother or Aunt Betty would resume their normal volume as they talked to Joanna's mother.

". . . should be sitting up by now."

". . . did the doctor say?"

"When Joanna was that age . . ."

Joanna began to understand that the grownups weren't all that happy with Molly. It didn't seem fair to be saying things about such a little baby who might not even know what it was people wanted. It finally occurred to Joanna that it was going to be up to her to let her sister know what was what. On a day when the comments about Molly had been particularly critical, Joanna got up off her bed, where she had been pretending to read, and crossed the room to her sister's crib. Molly, seeing Joanna, gave her radiant, toothless grin.

"Listen," Joanna said, putting her face up against the crib bars, "You're supposed to be doing stuff. Sit up, Molly."

Molly continued to beam at her sister, who reached an arm through the crib bars. The arm wasn't quite long enough to fit under Molly and lift her—Joanna looked around for something to climb on. Just then she heard her mother coming. She backed away from the crib, but not before whispering urgently to the baby.

"You'd better start doing *something*, Molly. They're waiting."

The waiting didn't last very long. Molly was fourteen months old, diagnosed as "severely retarded" (euphemisms such as "developmentally delayed" had not yet been coined), when Joanna's parents placed their younger daughter in an institution. They might have kept her at home, but by that time the placidity of Molly's infancy was long gone. She had become willful and aggressive and would slap at people when they tried to feed or dress her, or carry her where she didn't want to go. She would pull Joanna's hair as hard as she could. The first time it happened Joanna pulled right back, but was stopped by her mother's angry voice.

"Honestly, Joanna! She doesn't know any better—you do."

It took the heart out of Joanna's mother to "put Molly away," as Grandma and Aunt Betty referred to it. Joanna remembered the long car ride, and the sight of her mother wracked with tears as she handed her baby, all dressed up as if for Easter, to a woman in a white nylon uniform. The woman, whose eyes also looked wet, said to Joanna's mother, "We'll take good care of little Mary."

"Molly!" said Joanna's mother. "Her name is Molly."

Molly herself did not react to her mother's distraught voice. She lay passively against the breast of this complete stranger who couldn't even get her name right. Joanna's mother made a choked sound and ran from the baby-building (there were separate facilities for older children, and for grown-ups). Joanna remembered later that her mother had been bent nearly double with weeping, and her pretty, soft face had looked like that of a mad old woman. She was thirty-four—younger than Molly was now.

Nobody had expected Molly to live very long. Doctors told Joanna's parents that with all her health problems, including a serious heart murmur, Molly's life expectancy was twenty years, at most. Now here she was two decades later, forty years old with a mental age of four. Both her parents were dead, and come what may, she was Joanna's responsibility—the baby sister who had gotten bigger, but not older.

The elevator buttons read 1, 2, and Service. Joanna hesitated, then pushed the Service button, which logic dictated must be for the third floor. The elevator did go up, and Joanna got off it on a quiet floor that seemed poorly lit in comparison to the rest of the hospital. There was no nurses' station, but off to her left Joanna saw a desk, at which a nurse sat reading. The nurse looked up as if spooked. "Yes?" she said warily. "May I help you?"

"Mary Peters," said Joanna. "I'm her sister."

"Oh," said the nurse, and belatedly smiled. Always defensive on the subject of Molly, Joanna read into the smile: Poor Molly. Poor sister.

"We have her in that third room down," the nurse said, pointing. Joanna looked and saw light coming from the room. The nurse said brightly, "She has her very own private room."

Joanna had to admire the nurse's effort. Of course Molly had a private room, although the insurance only paid for a semi-private. Who would want to share a room with an adult-sized baby who gargled her few words and tossed around in the bed groaning and left the bathroom door open no matter how many times she was reminded.

It occurred to Joanna that this dimly-lit, unpopulated floor was probably used for non-violent prisoners and people in detox and other suffering souls who didn't enhance the image of the hospital as a bright, hopeful place where you went to get well. Sure enough—there were bars on the windows. Discreet, but definitely bars.

The nurse had started to get up, but stopped when Joanna said, "It's fine—I'll go in to her myself. She knows who I am."

The nurse sat back down and said in an apologetic tone, "I couldn't get her to eat. I covered up her dinner so I could try again later."

"It's fine," Joanna said again. This time she remembered to smile as she turned and walked toward Molly's room.

Joanna wondered what condition she would find Molly in. The call from Ben, who worked at the group home where Molly lived, had not been long on details. Molly had had a cough for most of the winter, but on the previous day she hadn't been able to stop hacking and could scarcely get her breath. Ben drove her to the emergency ward of this hospital, the nearest one to Molly's day program. The doctor on call, unable to get any information out of Molly, decided it would be prudent to admit her.

Entering Molly's room, Joanna saw her sister in a white bed with the side rails up. The head of the bed had been elevated, probably so the nurse could feed Molly, whose head was turned toward the dark, snow-spattered window. Joanna said softly, "Molly. Molly, honey."

Molly turned slowly and looked at her sister. Her jaw slackened and it seemed for a moment that she might speak. But instead she stretched out her right arm, with the palm of her hand turned up, and beckoned to Joanna. It was an oddly Sibylline gesture, and Joanna chose to take it as a welcome.

"Hi, Molly!" Joanna said, in an enthusiastic tone. She reached over the bed rail and gave her hand to Molly, who patted it absently. She was already looking out the window again. This almost non-existent attention span had been one of the first signs that there was something seriously wrong with Molly as a child.

"Molly," said Joanna, switching to a brisk, decisive tone, "What about your dinner! Do you want Jojo to feed you?"

Anyone overhearing might have thought that "Jojo" had been Molly's baby-name for her older sister. In fact, the name had been brother Danny's invention. The family would have been thrilled if Molly had ever come up with anything so normal.

"OK," Joanna said, as if Molly had answered. She reached over to the bedside table and lifted the aluminum cover from Molly's dinner, which consisted of a greenish-yellow mush. Bad teeth had been another early sign.

"Here we go," Joanna said. "Open up, Molly." Molly turned her head and opened her mouth very wide, showing her limp tongue and missing teeth. Joanna spooned in a bite of the mush and Molly chewed it loudly. After two more bites Molly pushed the spoon away and folded her arms across her chest—a gesture of refusal she had probably learned from Joanna.

"All done!" Joanna said, dabbing at Molly with a napkin as Molly struggled to avoid having her face washed. "There—nice and clean. Do you want to see what I brought you?"

This Molly understood. She reached across the bars for Joanna's yellow silk scarf, and yanked.

"Molly, no!" Joanna said, then more softly, "Silly Molly. You don't want Jojo's scarf. *This* is for you."

Now Molly's eyes were eager as she watched Joanna reach down and produce the tissue-wrapped present. When the toy was handed to her, Molly tore at the paper and uncovered a small patch of the stuffed toy. "Mine!" she said.

"Yes!" Joanna said, reaching over to help with the paper. Molly pulled her prize back. "Mine!" she said angrily.

"Oh, all right," Joanna sighed. "Do you like it Molly? That's for Molly's birthday."

Molly looked from the toy, which was still mostly wrapped, to her sister, and gave the package a possessive shake. Her face broke into a huge grin. "Bir-day," she said.

Joanna's eyes stung. For forty years her hopes had lifted whenever Molly made some simple connection like this. She said,

"That's right, honey. It's Molly's birthday. When you get out of the hospital we'll have a cake. And ice cream, Molly."

But Molly's interest had faded. She looked away, and tossed the toy toward the foot of the bed. "Bir-day," she said, and Joanna had to face the fact that the word, like most words, had no special meaning for her sister. Joanna had spent a lifetime insisting to other people that Molly understood things, while knowing perfectly well that she didn't.

Joanna stood, retrieved the stuffed toy and handed it back to Molly. When Molly didn't take her present Joanna put it next to her on the pillow. Their hands touched, and Molly again patted her sister's hand, then squeezed it, quite hard. Joanna said, "What, Molly? What do you want?" There was no answer, of course, and after a minute Molly withdrew her hand and flapped it toward the door. It was time for Joanna to leave. Joanna kissed her sister and walked to the doorway. She turned, expecting Molly to be staring out the window again, but Molly was looking right at her, as if waiting for something. Joanna started again to ask what Molly wanted, but then Molly raised her arm and waved it languidly, up and down. "Bye," she said. "Bye, Molly."

"Yes," said Joanna, her eyes prickling again. "That's *good*. Bye to Molly for now, and then tomorrow we'll have a party. For Molly's birthday." Joanna backed out of the room, waving until she was several steps down the corridor.

She was emotionally exhausted when she got home—a not unusual reaction to any length of time spent with Molly. She fed the cat, heated up some soup, and tried to watch a little television, but found the programs loud and irritating. At a little after ten she turned down the heat and went to bed, setting her alarm for a half-hour earlier than usual. Tomorrow was an important day at work.

Joanna was an assistant actuary for a large insurance company. She had actually started college as an English major, and it was with a pang for the disappointment she would bring her mother that she changed the focus of her studies. It had always made her mother happy to see Joanna being careful with books. Molly was murder on books, chewing them, breaking their spines, ripping out the pages. You had to hide anything you didn't want destroyed.

But then Joanna took a course in statistics, because it met a requirement and was scheduled at a good time. She loved it. Here was order, predictability—a way to improve the chances of knowing how things were going to turn out. She talked to a course counselor and by the next semester had a courseload of math, economics, and probability theory.

The morning after Joanna's visit to the hospital, an important client was coming in for a presentation. Joanna knew that her own large role in the upcoming meeting had to do in part with her being a woman. The client was young, and the firm was eager to be seen as progressive. Whatever the reason, Joanna was pleased with the recognition and had worked hard on her charts and her explanatory notes. Everything was in her briefcase, she was dressed in a stylish gray suit, and as planned she was at the office a good two hours before the scheduled meeting.

Joanna's routine on a day like this was to carefully go over her notes one final time, then put everything away a half hour before the meeting and turn her attention to something else. At 9:45 she was chatting with a colleague about a new movie when she remembered that she still had to call Molly's group home about the party Joanna had promised her sister. It would be a simple affair—cake and ice cream and Happy Birthday—but it wouldn't do to set it up if the guest of honor was not going to be released from the hospital today. Joanna considered calling the hospital but she didn't have the time to be put on hold, and instead dialed the number of the home.

"Hello—Mills House." The familiar voice sounded different. Joanna said, "Ben?"

"It's me," the voice said. "Joanna?"

"Yes. Do you have a cold?" Ben could be quite lengthy on the subject of his many real or imagined ailments so Joanna went on quickly, "Ben, I'm calling about Molly . . ."

"I just heard," Ben said, and began to cry. Joanna felt shock, then dread. "Heard what, Ben?"

"She passed away," Ben said, through his sobbing. "The hospital just called."

Joanna watched her left hand begin to shake. She pressed it onto the desk and made her voice very calm. "Ben, I saw Molly last night. They were going to let her go home today."

"They just called," Ben insisted. "They said her heart went into some . . . I don't know the word. It started beating like crazy and then it just stopped."

For a minute Joanna let him cry. Ben was overly emotional and a hypochondriac, but Molly's face always lit up at the sight of him. Then she said, "Ben, I'm going to have to hang up now and call the hospital. Is that . . . where she is?"

"I don't know," Ben sniffled. "I guess so."

"OK," Joanna said. "I'll take care of it, Ben. You try to calm down."

Joanna hung up and saw that the trembling in her hand had stopped. She took several deep breaths and straightened the papers on her desk. She walked to the door of her boss's office and knocked.

"Mr. Fuller? I'm sorry. It's Molly."

At the hospital, Joanna stood just inside the entrance in a state of indecision that was unlike her. Where was Molly? Certainly not in the little room on the third floor. Maybe—downstairs? Joanna walked to the information desk which, she saw to her relief, was staffed by a middle-aged woman who looked both efficient and approachable.

"Hello," Joanna said, as the woman smiled at her. "My name is Joanna Peters. I need to talk to somebody about my sister."

"Name?" said the woman, fingers ready over the computer keys.

"Peters—the same as mine. But she might not be in there. The person who called said she . . . died."

The woman's hands froze above the keyboard and she looked sharply at Joanna. "Oh . . ." she said, and then, "I'm sorry."

"Thank you," Joanna said, and waited while the woman made a call.

"Somebody's going to call me right back," the woman said. "Do you need to sit down, hon?"

"Oh—no. Thank you," Joanna said, but even as she said it a woozy, disoriented feeling came over her. She walked carefully to a row of bolted-down chairs and took the nearest one. The woman at the desk was watching her, and Joanna managed a smile which she hoped was reassuring. The phone rang, and the woman spoke into it for a minute, then called over to Joanna, "They'll come get you." Five minutes later a pretty young black woman in a pantsuit and light blue smock walked up to the receptionist, who pointed out Joanna. The black woman smiled.

"Ms. Peters? I'm Doctor Fredericks. Could we talk in my office?"

Joanna got up and followed the doctor to the elevators. They rode up to the second floor and walked down a corridor to a tiny private office with a desk and two visitor chairs. The doctor took one of the visitor chairs and Joanna took the other.

"First," the doctor said, "please accept my sympathy on your sister's death. I had actually just examined her and was only a few rooms away when it happened. Her heart went into tachycardia." She looked to see if Joanna was following what she was saying.

"Her heart speeded up to a rate of several hundred beats per minute—that's about five times a normal heart rate. She was in cardiac arrest by the time I got back to her room."

Joanna nodded, and asked, "Did she suffer?" She knew it was a question to which there would be only one answer, but she wanted to hear it.

"No," the doctor said. "She wouldn't have felt anything. It all happened in less than a minute."

Joanna sat looking down, thinking she ought to have something to say. She was responsible for Molly, after all. The doctor asked, "Do you have any questions?"

"No," Joanna said. "Thank you. I mean, thank you for taking care of her. I know you did everything you could."

"We did," the doctor said, "but I appreciate your saying it. You'll be the person responsible for making funeral arrangements?"

"Yes," Joanna said. "Actually, it's pretty much done. I pre-paid everything, and wrote it all out, just in case I wasn't around when Molly . . ."

The doctor nodded. "Yes—that was a good idea." She stood, and gave a pat to Joanna's shoulder. "Why don't you use the phone in here to make your calls, and I'll check back in with you in ten minutes or so."

The call to the funeral home went smoothly. The person who took the call was all business, his expression of sympathy neither perfunctory nor fulsome. He told Joanna that a vehicle would be sent for "the deceased," and that Joanna could come by the funeral home later in the day to answer a few questions about the notice that would go in the newspaper.

"There is one other thing," the man said. "Will you be bringing garments for your sister to wear?"

Joanna had not thought of that. Ben had picked out most of Molly's clothes, so that she had a collection of Hawaiian shirts and pants in purple or bright plaids.

"I guess I'll have to get her something," Joanna said. "What would you . . ." Again, she was at a loss for words.

"Well," the man said, in his assured but respectful tone. "We can be of assistance there, if you wish. We do have some very nice garments that we could choose from for you. Did Ms. Peters have a favorite color?"

Joanna felt a sense of unreality. This was like a daydream of hers that had persisted for years. In the dream, Molly had been normal, and she and Joanna had been TV-sisters, holding onto each other's arms while they gossiped about their double-dates, going to lunch and splitting a dessert, shopping for Molly's prom dress.

"Pink, I guess," Joanna said. She had no idea whether Molly had had a favorite color, but some instinct led her to choose a little girl's color.

"A nice choice for a young woman," the man said. Joanna knew she could have asked for orange or lime-green and he would have agreed, but probably with a gentle hint of regret that her choice was not in keeping with the solemnity of the occasion.

They set a time for Joanna to come by the funeral home, and she hung up. That was it for her calls. She'd wait until she was home to call Aunt Betty, and as for Danny, Joanna hadn't had an address for him in over ten years. Joanna remembered that she was supposed to wait for the doctor to come back, and hoped it wouldn't be too long. There was a pad on the desk and several pens, and Joanna made a few notes for the newspaper.

Mary Constance Peters. Age 40. *No education. No career. No husband, children, in-laws, pets. No hobbies or favorite charities.* Leaves a brother, sister and aunt. Joanna wondered how she was going to be able to get a paragraph out of Molly's life. Well, let the newspaper handle it. They must do it all the time.

There was a tap on the partially closed door, and the doctor came back in. She was carrying a white plastic bag with the name of the hospital on it in green. She said, "Were you able to make your calls?"

"Yes," Joanna said, standing. "I used a sheet of your paper. I hope that was all right."

"Of course," the doctor said. "Do you need to talk to anyone—a counselor?"

Joanna wondered if she seemed like a pretty cold fish, taking her sister's death so calmly. She supposed a reaction would set in later. She said, "No, thank you. You've been very kind."

The doctor said, "I've brought you these." She gestured with the bag. "These are the things Mary had with her."

Joanna took the bag, and looked inside. Molly's clothes were there, her orthopedic shoes, a few rolled-up magazines, and the purple stuffed pig. Joanna reached into the bag and took out the pig. It still had most of the wrapping paper on it.

"That's quite a color," the doctor said. "I'll bet she liked that."

"Oh, she did," Joanna said. "She loved purple." She put the pig back into the bag and neatly rolled the top. As she turned to go, Joanna covered for Molly one last time.

"She was really excited. No one could say she didn't know it was her birthday."

RENDEZVOUS

$\mathcal{T}$he President's staff, hoping for a sunny day, had been monitoring the weather since early morning. There was still a chance it could clear, but for now it didn't look too promising. Rain streaked the windows of the Hotel Texas, and it appeared that the crowd waiting in Dallas might not get the hoped-for glimpse of President and Mrs. Kennedy. The bubble top to the car was clear, but it wouldn't be the same as getting to see the attractive, youthful couple waving, Jack with his thick brown hair and famous smile. Kennedy needed Texas for his '64 run for re-election—it would mean a lot if the crowd could get a good view of Governor Connally and his wife in the motorcade, and their fellow Texan Lyndon Johnson in the Vice President's car.

The President's party was coming out of the hotel now, and agents hurried to open the doors of the waiting cars. During the drive to the airport, the weather began to look a little better. The rain lightened, and there were even a few breaks in the clouds. Mrs. Kennedy was able to stand in the open while cameras snapped and the President made his remarks. You had to admire the couple's style. Jackie so elegant, but with an appealing air of shyness, Jack charming the crowd with his inimitable gift of appearing to be among friends. The November sun was glinting on the President's hair and on Jackie's bright pink suit. If only this weather would hold.

In Dallas, the President's party was mobbed again, and Jackie was presented with an armful of bright red roses that glowed against her pink jacket. The motorcade formed and moved slowly out—a police car, the President's car, a car preceding the one in which the Johnsons were riding, and a caravan of other vehicles stretching behind the Vice President's convertible. The roaring from the huge crowd began at once. The Kennedys and the Connallys went to work grinning and waving. Little attention was paid to the Governor and his wife—all eyes were on the President and First Lady. The President had the motorcade stop twice so that, under the nervous eyes of his agents, he could shake hands.

Now the motorcade was entering Dealey Plaza. There were fewer police here—only a scattered crowd lined the short zigzag turn. The lead car came out of the turn and picked up speed as it moved toward the triple underpass.

Everyone's attention was focused on the second car—no one was watching the sky, where clouds had gathered. The clap of thunder took everyone by surprise. Right behind the loud noise came a burst of rain.

The onlookers, even as they scrambled for shelter or pulled up collars, moaned in disappointment. The security people looked relieved. An aide leaned into the car and spoke to the President, who ran his hand through his hair and pointed to his wife. Both Jack and Jackie waved vigorously one last time to the cheering crowd as men surrounded the dark blue Lincoln and snapped on the plastic top. The car moved slowly forward, following the lead car into the underpass.

"That feel better, Jackie?" The President asked his wife. "Nice and cool in here."

Jackie smiled at him. She had dressed wrong for the late Fall weather in Texas, and was suffering in the beautiful pink suit. She had not been sleeping well on the trip, and knew this was partly because it had only been three months since they lost Patrick, but she was glad she had come.

"It is better," she said. "I can't wait to get inside the dining room. I hope the air-conditioning is *freezing*."

The Lincoln pulled to a stop in front of the Trade Mart at 12:38. Only eight minutes behind schedule.

Secret Service men, holding umbrellas, shielded the occupants from the rain as they climbed out of the car. Jackie started to reach back for the bouquet of red roses, and an aide leaned close to speak to her.

"You may want to leave those, Mrs. Kennedy. It'll be all yellow ones inside."

As they entered, an organist played Hail to the Chief and everyone stood. The President and his wife were escorted to the head table, with people clapping on all sides. So many people, Jackie included, had been afraid of the Dallas trip, but it seemed that Nellie Connally had been right. Dallas loved JFK.

The meal was served as soon as the President was seated. There were two more motorcades to follow, and every minute counted. Jackie sat enjoying the coolness, smiling at everyone and trying to make her soft voice heard whenever she was asked a question. The President wasn't getting a chance to eat his lunch, but there was still a reception in Austin, followed by dinner.

The introduction concluded, and Jack got up to speak. Even after more than a decade, Jackie's attention never wandered when her husband gave a speech. The words themselves were always good, but it was Jack's delivery—the charm, the Boston accent, the familiar gestures—that so captivated his audience.

". . . For as was written long ago: 'Except the Lord keep the city, the watchman waketh but in vain' . . ." the President said. His voice dropped, and the applause began and went on and on.

As Jackie rested back at the hotel, she could hear her husband and his aides in the next room, planning, disputing, all talking at once. What energy they had. Jackie closed her eyes, knowing she would need her own energy for the evening festivities.

She was awakened by her personal assistant, who had already drawn a bath and laid out a white dress. The pink suit was gone, and Jackie reminded herself never to wear it again in hot weather. When she had finished dressing and every hair was in place, she went out into the suite's living room to meet her husband.

"Jackie!" the President said. "You look beautiful."

"And you look very handsome, Mr. President," she said, smiling. He was wearing a blue suit and red tie, and his eyes glowed with the success of the trip so far. The Secret Service was right at hand, but grew deaf when Jackie leaned in for a private word with her husband.

"I was so worried about today," she said. "All those warnings and the signs and that article in the paper this morning . . . ."

"I know," he said. His voice was gentle, as it so often was since Patrick. "But the way I look at it, when it's your time it's your time. It will be someday, Jackie, but not this trip." He smiled, just for her. "I'm glad you're with me."

The reception was at the Governor's mansion, and both Kennedys were swept into a whirl of introductions, handshakes, and touches. It was as if anyone who came into contact with the beautiful couple would take home a small share of the magic. At dinner, Jackie got to see again the class with which her husband could handle a tricky situation. It seemed that only belatedly had the menu planners realized they shouldn't have decided to serve steak on a Friday night. Kennedy was, after all, a practicing Catholic. Whispered conversations and apologies ran along the head table until they reached the President himself.

"When in Texas . . ." he said gallantly, and cut a large piece of his steak.

Jackie smiled at his tact and looked again at her program. *This is a day to be remembered in Texas*, read the greeting from the Governor.

It was nearly eleven o'clock when the party reached the Johnson ranch. Lady Bird, clucking in a motherly fashion, hustled Jackie off to a waiting guest room. As the two women started up the staircase, Jackie looked back at her husband, surrounded as always and gesturing with his Scotch. Jack looked up, and gave her a full, dazzling smile before turning his head to whoever had just spoken to him.

In the morning, Jackie slept later than usual. Campaigning certainly took a lot out of you, and this was only the beginning. When she came down to breakfast, casually but beautifully dressed, Jack was having coffee with the Johnsons and his closest aides. He grinned at his wife.

"Jackie!" he said in his high-spirited way. "You'll need to change as soon as you've had breakfast. Lyndon's got some horses he wants us to try."

Jackie brightened. She loved riding, and seldom had a chance to do it with her husband. She said, "You can wear your new hat."

Everybody laughed. At the breakfast in Fort Worth, Jack had been given a tan Stetson. Here in the privacy of his Vice-President's home, he could wear it without wondering whether someone would snap an unflattering photograph in which he would look foolish.

"I will," Jack said. "Bring it down for me after you've changed."

Jackie breakfasted, then went upstairs and put on riding clothes. The hat was on the dresser, and she brought it back downstairs and held it out it to her husband.

"Here," she said. "Allow me."

He ducked his head so she could place the hat on him, and as he straightened up he kissed her.

"Let's go," he said. "Let's see if Lyndon knows anything about horses."

"I heard that," the Vice-President said, and led the way to the stables.

From the barn, a young woman in jeans was leading out a glossy-coated chestnut horse. The animal was stocky in appearance, with a placid expression and a steady, slightly rolling gait. Behind it, a second stable hand held the reins of a black horse.

"Tennessee Walkers," Johnson said proudly. "Jackie—" he indicated the chestnut mare—"I know what a rider you are, so this one's yours. The big black fellow is reserved for those of us who do most of our riding in limos."

The plan was for a short ride along trails shaded by live oaks. The Secret Service fanned out so as to give the President's party a little privacy, but still be ready to move in a hurry if they were needed. The President's horse had taken the lead, lifting and setting down its hooves in a characteristic flat-footed walk. The riders came out from under the shade of an enormous tree into bright sunlight—and the black horse screamed.

For a breath, everyone was paralyzed. Then one of the Secret Service men shouted, "Rattler!" The snake was coiled just beneath the horse's right foreleg. Guns were waving, trying to aim for the snake without endangering the horse. The rattler drew back, and a second before the first shots, he struck.

The horse made a terrible sound, and reared up. The President was struggling to hold on—they were almost to him. Then the horse, blind with panic, swung in a circle and the President's body rose over the animal's head. The Secret Service, knocking into one another, were close enough to touch him as he landed.

He lay on his back, the hat next to him, his arms flung out. People were shouting orders and kneeling beside him. More people were running from the house. Jackie's Secret Service agents surrounded her as she sat shaking on her horse, her hands covering her mouth.

"Mrs. Kennedy," an agent said, reaching for the trailing reins. "We need to get you back inside. They're taking care of the President."

She looked at him with eyes that were huge, outraged, changed. She had seen the impossible angle of the President's neck and she knew—they all did. It was here and now. It was today.

THE WAY OUT

*L*ucy can't imagine how couples who hate each other ever get through it all. This journey's end, with a vocabulary all its own. *Irretrievable breakdown. A growing estrangement which has become intolerable.* And the most bloodless one of all, stark and formal, *issue,* meaning children.

But getting through it they are, she and John, dividing up money and property, filling out brightly colored forms required before the Commonwealth of Massachusetts will officially dissolve their union. And today, to add his certification to yet more documents, a notary public.

Lucy has been the one to call around and find a notary who works Saturdays. John is picking Lucy up here, at the home that is now hers alone. She keeps going to the window to see if her—what?—has arrived, and when he does pull into the driveway, she backs quickly away from the window, as if guilty of something. She stands expectantly near the door for a moment before she remembers that John has no key.

"I'm a little early," John says, when she lets him in. "I forgot there wouldn't be the weekday traffic." He stands awkwardly just inside the back door, holding his briefcase.

"Oh, it's fine," Lucy says, trying for lightness. She is still unaccustomed to the lack of names, endearments, touching. "It gives us time for coffee. Unless you want to stop on the way . . ."

John looks around doubtfully. He has been uncomfortable in the house since signing it over to Lucy. He looks at the things he has chosen or installed or repaired, then says, "Sure. Here would be fine." His voice is strained—Lucy turns away from the sound of it.

They sit at the kitchen table, giving their attention to the coffee, not speaking. At last John sets down his still half-full mug. "We should go."

Lucy listens for a moment to the voice inside her head. *No,* it is saying. *I don't want to. I won't.*

"I'll get my purse," she says.

They take John's truck, and he drives while Lucy reads from the directions. They pass a failing strip mall, a lumberyard, a discount food warehouse, and there ahead of them is the sign for Country Living Estates. John puts on his blinker and turns onto the treeless road that winds into the development.

Lucy wonders what John is thinking. Another thing she is not used to is the absence of silliness between them, the shared jokes about a place like this, in all its horribleness. The development consists of what seems to be hundreds of mobile homes on small slabs, each only a few yards from its neighbor and each painted yellow, white or gray. The streets are all named for trees—Lucy watches carefully for Linden.

"That must be him," John says.

Beneath the sign for Linden Street a man is smiling and waving. Lucy hears John sigh—a just-our-luck sigh. She supposes John was hoping for a dour, even impatient notary who would have them in and out.

"You made it," the man calls as Lucy gets out of the truck and John follows, looking reluctant. "Any trouble finding the place?"

"No," Lucy says. "The directions were fine. We're a few minutes early . . ."

The man, who has started back toward his house, waves dismissively. Lucy looks at John, who shrugs, and they follow the man inside.

The house is tiny, cluttered with furniture and knick knacks. A few steps take Lucy, John, and the notary through the living room and into a dining area with a maple table and three captain's chairs. The notary indicates where everyone is to sit, then goes back into the living room and opens the top drawer of a glass hutch filled with commemorative plates. From the drawer he takes a leather case and brings it back to the dining area. He pulls a bright stamp from the case and places it on the table, where it looks serious and professional.

"Now," says the notary "What have you folks got for me?"

Lucy suppresses a sigh. She has explained things carefully on the telephone, in the interests of making this ordeal as brief as possible. John answers for them both.

"It's an affidavit and a separation agreement," John says. "We need you to witness and notarize our signatures."

The notary nods, looking grave, as if he is being asked to do something out of the ordinary, or not quite legal. When he doesn't say anything, John says, "Perhaps we could start with my . . . with my wife's affidavit."

He looks at Lucy, who opens her folder and takes out the single cream-colored document that it contains. The notary takes it from her and reads it thoroughly. Finally he slides it back to her, pointing to where she should sign. Lucy is going to keep John's last name, and she feels relief that she is not signing it for the last time. John touches her hand. He points out that Lucy had been about to enter the date on the line reserved for the notary's use.

Lucy nudges the affidavit back across the table and again the notary studies it. Lucy can feel John's impatience ticking away beside her and she is about to speak when at long last the notary positions the gold circle of foil and presses the double handles on his stamp. "Can't get used to writing 2000," he says as he fills in the year his commission will expire. He hands the affidavit, with its few stray marks, back to Lucy and turns to John. "You got one of these, too?"

John doesn't understand for a moment. Then he says, "Yes. But the only other thing we need is for you to witness both our signatures on the separation agreement."

John sounds curt, and seems to realize it. His fair skin colors and he reaches into his folder for his own affidavit and shows the notary that it has already been witnessed and stamped.

The notary examines the document. "Who's she?" he asks.

"She," John says, "is a notary in Springfield. Could we get on to the separation agreement, please? I have to be somewhere."

The notary reaches for the document on which John has typed both his and Lucy's names, and Lucy's heart sinks as he settles in to read it. Lucy sees that John is about to say something, but just then the notary turns the document at an angle and points.

"This date here," he says. "That's 1967?"

The date is typed, so Lucy knows there is no confusion arising from John's habit of putting a horizontal line across the number 7. She says, "Yes, June 26, 1967. It's the date of our marriage."

"Twenty nine years," says the notary.

"Twenty eight," says John. "Could we . . ."

The notary sits back, and folds his arms. His expression is paternal.

"Look," he says. "Have you kids really thought this through?"

Lucy and John are speechless. She recovers first.

"Of course we have," she tells the notary. "Thought it through." Before John can break in she adds, "It's been very difficult. We . . . I'd appreciate it if you could just finish these papers for us."

The notary looks sad. He shakes his head slightly and reaches for his stamp. Lucy watches, scarcely breathing, as the notary impresses his seal on the separation agreement and fills out the remaining lines.

"I'm a justice of the peace, too," he says, sliding the notarized agreement into the neutral area between John and Lucy. "I marry folks right here in this room. I like that part. This part I don't like, but what can you do."

Lucy can't imagine what this impossible man wants from them. Isn't this against the code of ethics for notaries? Is he waiting for a cinematic moment of reconciliation? Lucy says a little desperately, "How much do we owe you?"

The notary sighs. "Usually I charge five dollars apiece. But why don't we call it eight dollars for both? I don't make my living this way."

Lucy doesn't doubt that statement. This misbegotten optimist probably marries people for free. She hands him a ten dollar bill, and he takes a tan wallet from his pocket and carefully makes change. John, now that the services have been paid for, reaches for the separation agreement and slips it into his folder.

"Lucy," John says, "I need yours, too. To file on Monday." She holds out the folder to him, and John removes the affidavit and hands the empty folder back.

"Don't forget about copies," the notary says. Lucy is relieved that he seems to have accepted the fact that he is abetting a divorce. "I always make copies, even when I'm just writing to my boys."

"We will," Lucy says. "Thank you. Thank you for seeing us on Saturday."

John is already at the door. The notary places a hand near Lucy's elbow like a Boy Scout helping a frail old lady across the street. They reach the door and he leans past John to work a burglar-friendly lock.

"It's finicky," he says as the door swings open. "Needs a little oil, I guess."

John is walking quickly toward the truck and Lucy has a moment of wishing that he had been the one to take her arm. She says again, "Thank you," and the notary responds, "That's what I'm here for. I'm in the book, if you need me again."

Need him again? How many twenty-eight-year divorces did this fellow think she had in her. Or maybe he thought she'd be back soon with her new man, ready to tie the knot in front of those commemorative plates from all over America. Lucy walks around the front of the truck and gets in the passenger side, and John starts the engine before she has finished fastening her seat belt. The notary is standing on the grass waving goodbye, but Lucy has no free hand to return the gesture.

When Lucy has finally gotten her seat belt buckled, she looks back and sees the notary still watching them, his hand dropped to his side. She gives a laugh that is not far from hysteria. John looks at her with consternation, then grins.

"I was waiting to meet the missus," he says.

"She would have given us coffeecake," Lucy says shrilly. "We would have looked at pictures of the grandkids. She would have told us to call her Mamie."

This foolishness sets them both off, and Lucy laughs until she is crying. Through her tears she sees John's fifty-year-old face and it is the face of the boy she married. How she had loved that boy. How her life, as young as his, had revolved around their shared sorrows and joys.

"Oh, no," John says. It is almost a moan, and Lucy looks around in alarm. She sees that they are passing the notary's house again, and he is still standing on his lawn.

"We went in a circle," John says. "I don't believe this." Just as he says this, the notary moves toward the truck. John accelerates as Lucy waves and grins, indicating with sign language that they are fine—not lost at all.

And, a minute later, they aren't. Lucy recognizes a cast-iron rooster that they passed on the way in, and John takes the fork he missed when they were both laughing. There is a sign reading Way Out, and Lucy says, "We must not be the only ones to have that problem."

Traffic noise rises from the highway as they round a last curve and John slows for the stop sign. Lucy wonders how long the notary will stand there in his yard before accepting that he has seen the last of them.

IMPEDIMENTS

$\mathcal{L}$ucy discovers the tape while getting the house ready to sell, five years after the divorce. The oversized plastic reel is more than thirty years old, the songs and poems on it now four hundred years old. Looking at the brown magnetic strip, Lucy can remember every detail of the day she and John recorded it. Is it still playable? Does she want to hear it?

Lucy at fifty-six, sorting and packing and discarding, tries to picture herself at twenty. The image is indistinct—a brown-eyed girl with long brown hair, neither short nor tall, dressed in the flowered cottons of that time. Imagine—she had no wrinkles, and not a single gray hair. When she turns her mind's eye to John, the past emerges more clearly. There are his curls, his blue eyes, the disarming sweetness of his smile. She listens, and seems to hear him singing.

The day they made the tape was not the first time she heard John sing. He was a regular at the campus coffeehouse, playing backup guitar for a self-important girl who was never heard from again after college. Sometimes he would join the lead singer on the choruses, his warm tenor giving new life to the predictable and overused songs about peace and love and riding the rails.

The idea for the tape came about when John and Lucy had been together for about six months, and she talked him into joining her in a Shakespeare course. The young professor was progressive—he didn't see why the class should limit itself to reading and discussing the plays. He proposed that the students should team up to produce "living" Shakespeare projects. Acting out scenes from the plays, perhaps, or designing costumes or stage sets.

"I signed up to read Shakespeare and what's-his-name—Harold Bloom," Lucy told John as they walked the campus path that led to the library. It was April, and the budding trees and Spring sun improved the looks of their perpetually underfunded state college. "If I wanted to act or paint scenery, I'd have signed up for a drama course."

John swung his book bag high in the air, from sheer energy. His jeans and denim jacket were as much a uniform as Lucy's flowered shifts and sandals. He said, "You have a nice speaking voice. You know how to . . . enunciate. How about if we tape some of the Sonnets, and the songs from the plays? I know you think you can't sing—" (she knew she couldn't) "—but I can." He gave her his wonderful smile. "We'll pool our talents."

John knew a man-about-campus who had keys to everything. Peter arranged for them to use a rehearsal room in the music department, on a Saturday night when no one was around. John set up the heavy reel-to-reel tape recorder and they tested the sound, making silly noises into the microphone and imitating the more pompous of their professors.

When they were ready, Lucy got out her underlined copy of the Sonnets and handed John the words to the songs they had selected. She had typed these in her dorm room, enchanted by the language and trying to imagine it set to music.

She went first, reading Sonnet 2. They had decided on a simple chronological approach, beginning with the sonnet cycle that urges a beautiful youth to marry and pass on his charms to his offspring.

When forty winters shall besiege thy brow,

And dig deep trenches in thy beauty's field . . .

Lucy was pleased with the sound of the poem when they played it back. Her voice seemed to have caught both the lilting rhythm and the undertone of warning. She went on to the next sonnet, then John sang several of the songs. After each recording, they played the tape back and complimented each other.

"You sound good."

"That chorus is just right."

They had decided to end with the song "Tell me where is fancy bred," from *The Merchant of Venice*. John had been singing, on and off, for two hours, with breaks for black coffee and Marlboros, but he was twenty years old. His voice rose in the practice room as sweet and fair as any Ariel's.

Tell me where is fancy bred,
Or in the heart, or in the head?
How begot, how nourish`ed?

Lucy, listening, felt tears rise. She wanted to marry that voice. She wanted to carry in her own unmusical body a boy or girl who would sing like that.

John wanted to make love in the practice room before they returned the key, but Lucy was afraid someone would come by. She convinced him to come back to her dorm room instead. Her roommate was in Binghamton, being a bridesmaid for a girl whose wedding had been moved up to before graduation.

Lucy and John didn't have to have a hurry-up wedding. They took precautions, and announced their engagement just before graduation. John was accepted to graduate school and Lucy, who had had enough of school, found a job editing press releases and a newsletter for a company that made upscale fruit juices.

Three years into the marriage, no boys or girls had arrived, musical or otherwise.

"Do you think we should get checked?"

Lucy looked at her husband over the top of the local paper. She had just read aloud a birth announcement, so John's question was not a *non sequitur*.

"Us? Why—I mean, we're only twenty-five. Besides, don't you like it to be just us for a while?"

"Well, sure. I just thought we might want to find out. In case there was anything we needed to . . . get used to."

Lucy smiled at him. "Why don't we give it a little more time? I promise—if we're pushing thirty and there's still no heir apparent, I'll go."

"We'll both go."

Shortly after Lucy's twenty-seventh birthday, she talked to a friend who had "been through it," and got the name of a specialist. Their first appointment was together, followed by separate sessions, presumably to encourage absolute candor. Then came the procedures, the waiting, and—symmetrically enough—a second joint appointment.

"What do you know," John said. "It's both of us."

Lucy was at a loss for words, which was probably a good thing. Whatever she said, it needed to be right. They were walking in a small park not far from the specialist's office. It was September, which at their age still felt like the start of the school year.

"And here I always thought we were perfect," John said.

Lucy felt her heart constrict. What that casual tone must be costing him . . . She took his hand and pressed it hard.

"We *are*. Oh, John, of course we are."

She started to say more, then thought better of it. Leave it. Leave it right there.

John's career rose. They never talked about it, but their childless state allowed them to take certain financial risks. No college to save for, no trips to Epcot. John entered into a partnership with a friend from graduate school who had his own software company. They were in the right place at the right time, doing young men's work. John no longer wore denim, except on weekends, but neither was he required to wear a suit to work.

Lucy, who had always enjoyed cooking, started a catering business. Before long, it outgrew her kitchen, and she rented space not far from John's office. They tried to meet at least once a week for lunch, but their schedules were hectic and seldom in sync. John was an only child, but on Lucy's side there were nieces and nephews. Her sister and brother expected that she would be a doting aunt, and were somewhat surprised when she was only affectionate and a little distracted around the younger generation.

The year they both turned thirty-five—"We're halfway through our three score and ten," said Lucy, the English major—they bought a summer house on Cape Cod. It needed work, inside and out, so weekends were spent in trips to the paint and hardware stores, and the garden center for shrubs and plants that would stand up to the Atlantic winds. The crab apple tree they planted in their small front yard survived, and after five years bore lumpy fruit from which Lucy made jam.

Sunday afternoons, with the luxury of waiting until Monday to leave the Cape, Lucy and John would often go into town to walk along the harbor, go to the bookstore, perhaps see a matinee at the movie theater that would close for the winter. They would end their day with dinner at their favorite restaurant, a restored stagecoach inn with sconces and period furniture and oil portraits of ruddy-faced sea captains. Lucy liked to order rice with her meal, to share with John, while he would get the French fries, knowing how Lucy loved the blackened ones he wouldn't eat.

Because they had been regulars for so long at the inn, Lucy and John had no trouble, even though it was the height of summer, reserving a private room for the celebration of their twenty-fifth anniversary. Friends and family gathered, some from long distances away, bringing the nieces and nephews, who had been forbidden for the evening the use of their Walkmans. There were toasts, good wishes, and presents, which Lucy and John opened together, exclaiming over the good choices their friends had made, how well they knew them both.

A few weeks before Lucy's fiftieth birthday, John asked if there was anything special she wanted, or wanted to do. She started to say no, intending to add that she had everything she wanted, but felt tears coursing down her face, amazing them both.

The talks started out almost shyly, then grew bolder as they discovered that, even in this, they had things in common.

"Not unhappy with *you*, of course . . ."

". . . still love you . . ."

"It's just that I'd always be wondering . . ."

Once, brushing at the tears that were as reliable as an allergy, Lucy said, "We're having our mid-life crises together. That's got to be something."

"My English major. She knows the plural of 'crisis'." John touched Lucy's damp face. "I know you don't like having to wear reading glasses, but I like the way you look in them." He took his hand away. "If . . ."

"If what?"

"Nothing."

Predictably, everyone said that John and Lucy were the last couple they ever expected to be getting a divorce. "Not you!" a friend cried in dismay. "We always thought . . ."

"Yes," Lucy said. "So did we."

All around them, couples their age were getting rancorous divorces. Fighting over houses, money, children. John and Lucy behaved with a courtesy and style that belied their sorrow. The house was hers now, so they met at restaurants (though not the inn). They were formal most of the time, only occasionally slipping into old habits. Once, John took a dark brown French fry from his plate and put it on Lucy's. She looked at it, then at him. He remembered.

Within just a year of their decision, it was done. Financial statements, notarized affidavits, a *decree nisi,* and a final decree. They kept in touch at first, but talked less often as each of them made new friends who hadn't known them as John and Lucy. The house on the Cape brought a good price, and since the two dogs were attached to each other, Lucy kept them both.

Now here is Lucy, holding in her hand a record of their beginnings, hers and John's. Of course she will play it. The ancient tape recorder is in a box of its own, padded with towels. Lucy finds a knife and cuts the strapping tape. Will both the player and the tape work? There is only one way to find out.

She takes the tape out of its box and threads it into the player. The PLAY button pops back up, but she presses it more firmly and the tape begins to turn. There is faint static, then—my God—her own voice, from more than half a lifetime ago.

She listens to the poems and songs, murmuring along with the ones she knows by heart. The tape reaches Lucy's final recitation, Sonnet 116.

> Let me not to the marriage of true minds
> Admit impediments; love is not love
> Which alters when it alteration finds
> Or bends with the remover to remove.

She has closed her eyes, and now opens them and reaches out to stop the tape. She—or rather, that girl of twenty—has tripped on a word. Impediments. She has missed the stress, and hurried ever so slightly on the last syllables. She rewinds, gets the end of a song, then her own reading again.

Yes, there it is. A catch, and then a beat of silence before her voice finds the rhythm and flows effortlessly to the final couplet.

Odd that she'd never noticed it. She had played the tape several times before handing it in to the teacher. If John noticed, he'd never said. Professor Burke had loved the project, and given them both an A. (Most of the class got an A, but it was nice for John, who was a history major.)

Lucy plays Sonnet 116 a final time. She is used to the slip now, and it sounds very slight in the echoing room, stacked with boxes. It is the very briefest of hesitations, caught in that other time. Too late to fix it now.

LAST LIGHT

*L*ucy thinks, *That can't be him.*

The bright yellow plane sweeps down the runway, propeller reversing, past the man waiting by the airstrip. Lucy glimpses a red face, bald head, stooped shoulders. The Henry she remembers is trim and full of vitality. But it's been twelve years—he has to be in his eighties, and of course he lost Gwen a year ago. Lucy feels herself fashioning an expression that will take no notice of the changes.

The pilot brings the plane out of its turn and cuts the engine. Lucy leans forward, eager for her first breath of the island's smell. It rushes in—spruce trees, rugosa, salt air—as the pilot opens his door and comes around to lower the steel steps. He hands a mail bag to the red-faced man, and Lucy, stepping from the plane, turns her smile on him.

"Lucy."

The voice is behind her. A trained, actor's voice. She would know it anywhere.

"Henry," she says, and turns to see a ghost. It is him, just as he was—sunburned and freckled, wearing chinos, a blue button-down shirt, and moccasins. His hair—if he still has it—is covered by a tan crushable hat, which just might be the same one he had the first time they met.

Henry reaches up and sweeps the hat from his head in a courtier's gesture. The hair, once red, is still there—long and wavy and white as snow.

"Oh, Henry," Lucy says, hurrying into his arms. "You look like King Lear."

On maps, the road that runs the length of the island is marked as Unimproved Dirt. Henry drives very slowly, but his truck has no shocks, and Lucy clings to the door to keep from hitting her head. The houses, boats and flowers, the graveyard they are passing, are as she remembers them, but it is an illusion. Henry tells her that the beautiful white house at the crossroads has stood empty since a teenager died there of a heroin overdose.

Henry turns just after his own house, down a grassy track with branches scraping the roof of the truck, and Lucy sees the A-frame. Its characteristic shape has been modified with dormers, but it is still the house she visits in her dreams. Lucy walks to the back of the truck to lift out one of her boxes, and follows Henry inside.

"Lots of changes," Henry says, setting the box of groceries on the kitchen counter. "We barely had electricity when you were coming here—" he gestures—"now there's a microwave and a gadget to grind the coffee beans." Lucy, who doesn't plan to make use of either of these wonders, is beginning to smile politely when she sees the mug.

It is on the draining board, upside down, the way she would have placed it all those years ago. A pale green ceramic mug with a thin white crack in the glaze. She used to bring John coffee in this mug, when he'd been up late looking through his telescope at the stars. Lucy's fingers flex, as if around the handle.

". . . plug this in?"

She looks from the cup to Henry. He is holding something made of beige plastic, with a dangling cord.

"The A-frame has a phone, Henry? Since when?"

"Oh, a few years now. Folks seem to want to keep in touch with what they're supposed to be getting away from."

John certainly did. Lucy remembers him, those last couple of years, walking the two miles to the harbor, where a telephone that ran on microwaves served as umbilical cord to his office.

"Thanks, Henry, but I . . . I'd like it if things could be the way they were."

Henry looks at the phone he is holding, utterly useless without its connection. Crossing the small room, he parts a mustard-colored curtain that conceals two rough shelves. With an air of ceremony, he nests the telephone in an open box of jigsaw puzzle pieces, tugs the curtain back into place, and bows.

After Henry leaves, Lucy goes out on the deck. She hadn't known—still doesn't—whether coming back here was a good idea. If Henry, so solid and familiar with his freckles and deep voice, seemed like a ghost, will John be haunting her everywhere?

Lucy unpacks, changes her shoes, and walks to the beach. No one is there to see her roll up her jeans and step into the gray surf, letting a wave break over her feet and ankles. The cold is numbing—she imagines liquid nitrogen would feel like this. Backing away from the water, she continues down the beach to the granite slope at the far end. She climbs the slope with more caution than she once did, and at the top sees The Loop, a wide circle through tall grass, along black cliffs, and back to the trees that enclose Henry's house. She and John got into the habit of walking this path at dusk, leaving a light on in the A-frame to guide them back through the dark woods.

Lucy steps onto the straight path. The Loop is for another day.

All week, the weather is divine. Garden of Eden weather, dry and sunny, seventy degrees in the daytime and sixty at night. Lucy begins each day under the island's spell of repose. She makes coffee, opens the windows, and reads in bed as the lobster boats head out. With the lifting of the morning fog, other islands appear on the horizon. She takes walks, stopping to admire the Fall flowers and migrating birds. One afternoon in the middle of the week, she visits the small graveyard and reads the carved names of people she knew. Most of them were Henry's age, but in the back corner under a catalpa tree is Elizabeth Hall. Lucy is startled, then saddened to see Elizabeth's name in this spot—they were the same age, and liked to talk about dogs and books.

After dinner each night, she reads *New Yorkers*, damp from the salt air and full of Presidential campaign news and speculation about which party will occupy the White House in the new century. At home, with the election imminent, Lucy and her friends have been arguing passionately about the candidates. But out here, under the wash of stars, she feels very removed from such fervor. In the sleeping bag she used to share with John, she is free from dreams.

It turns out that Henry is taking the plane back with Lucy on Saturday. He is going to be casting a Little Theater production of *Arsenic and Old Lace*. Lucy learns this in a way that is typical of communication on the island. She is out walking, her thoughts on the stunning Scarlet Tanager she has just seen, when Henry pulls up next to her and stops his truck in the middle of the road. It is a Stage Three island vehicle—the fuel pump has died, and a gas can mounted on a stick feeds gasoline to the carburetor through a scaly hose.

They talk for ten minutes with no other vehicle appearing on the road, then Henry asks, "Will you have High Tea with me?"

Lucy laughs. "You're forgetting I came here quite a few times. I'm onto you, Henry. High Tea means you need to use up everything in the refrigerator before you leave."

Henry grins at her. "Five P.M.," he says, and restarts the clattering engine.

The evening is cool as Lucy, in long pants and a sweater, walks to Henry's house. Passing Gwen's garden, in its September glory, she can almost see Gwen there weeding and watering, in a faded T-shirt printed with a map of the London subway. Henry has set everything out in front of a window that overlooks the islands, and now fills a kettle for tea. He and Lucy snack on cheeses, carrot sticks, celery, peanut butter, and crackers so soft they could be used for rollups. Lucy offers to help clean up, but Henry says, "No, you sit and enjoy the view. I'm getting used to these kitchen chores."

The sky is silver, the thickening dusk broken by the lights of a boat coming in. Lucy says, "You must miss her."

"Sometimes I'm mad at her. I know one of us had to go first, but I was planning on its being me. And the way she went—emphysema just ain't pretty." Henry's speech is always impeccable—the slang tells Lucy all she needs to know about the depth of his pain. Then he says, "And you?"

Lucy prods a soggy cracker to the edge of her plate. "Oh, it's not the same thing. Divorce and . . ." She can't come up with a word. Death? Being widowed? Losing someone who wanted to stay? Finally she says, "I thought it was going to be . . . hard . . . coming here without him, but it's not. It's just different."

"Different," Henry agrees. Then, "My son-in-law wanted me to go back with him yesterday. But that would have meant leaving you an island car. Zero to one mile an hour in fifteen minutes."

Lucy laughs, and her grandmother's expression comes to her. "Saints preserve us," she says.

It is almost fully dark when Lucy gets up to go. Henry wants to walk her back to the A-frame, but she says, hugging him, "No reason to let the mosquitoes feast on both of us."

"Need a flashlight?"

"Thanks—no. I took the one from next to the back door."

Henry stands in the doorway watching her go. When she reaches the roadway, he waves and turns back inside. The kitchen light goes out.

Lucy was wrong about the mosquitoes. It must be too dark for them to be out. The air feels wonderful, quite chilly now, rich with the island's special smell. Tomorrow, she will be back in her other world.

She knows that world—the mainland—is visible from the top of the cliffs. From the midpoint of The Loop.

Aiming her flashlight at the ground, she locates the mowed path. She follows it as it curves south and west, out of the trees toward the ocean she has been hearing grow louder. With her first sight of the phosphorescent waves, she is struck with a precise and vividly detailed memory.

John had taken his kayak out, and was late. She had gone to the top of the cliffs, as other women must have done before her, to watch for him. In the last light of that September day, the little red and white boat appeared on the horizon. The paddle rose and fell steadily, golden drops of water sheeting from it. The boat angled toward the beach, and Lucy climbed down to meet her husband.

They carried the kayak back together through the dark trees. Lucy never told John that she was worried. He was safe—that was all that mattered.

There is not a breath of wind, but Lucy shivers. The night holds her suspended, caught in a moment of perfect balance. Becalmed.

Wherever did that word come from? Something in mythology—ships that couldn't sail until the wind came up. Restless souls on board, waiting for the wind to rise and choose direction.

CROSSING THE DATELINE

*J*ohn has asked Lucy to meet him for lunch, at a restaurant close to the house Lucy is in the process of selling. Agreeing, she wonders if he is reluctant to see the house they shared stripped nearly clean, its contents boxed for Lucy's move to Maine.

"Can we make it one instead of noon?" she asks him. "I'm on a roll taking stuff to the dump."

The restaurant is several cuts above fast food, so Lucy changes out of the jeans and sweatshirt she has been living in, brushes back her short hair, and sets off to spend an hour with the man she once expected to be spending her life with.

John's truck, a gray Tacoma, is in the small parking lot, with John behind the wheel. He waves to Lucy and gets out of the truck to meet her. They hug—he presses for a moment into her neck—and say simultaneously, "You look well."

Lucy doesn't know or particularly care how she looks, but it is true that John looks better than the last time she saw him, several months ago. He has lost some weight, and his skin tone is less florid. She notices there's more gray in his hair (as in her own), but his is as thick and curly as it always was.

The hostess shows them to a table by the window, and they sit opposite each other looking like the married couple they were for close to thirty years. The divorce was almost six years ago, but as far as the remembered rituals are concerned, it's as if no time at all has intervened. Lucy, who is shorter than John, sits where the sun is on the top of her head but would have been in John's eyes. She moves her place setting next to the wall, and he follows suit.

"I've always liked this place," he says, looking around. "I wonder if they still have those string French fries."

"They do," Lucy says. "I had them last week."

He turns from the window. "You were here?"

Sometimes she wonders if he thinks she ceases to exist between the rare times when they are together.

"It was Eve's birthday. A group of us came here."

Eve is her friend from after the divorce. A number of people—couples for the most part—none too gradually counted Lucy out of their social circle when she became single. It hurt, and finding that she was capable of making a new close friend did much to bolster her spirits.

"What are you going to have?" John asks.

"Oh, the cheeseburger, I guess. With string fries. I know I shouldn't be eating like this, but I figure I need the calories. Moving is hard work."

"How's that going?"

"Oh, fine. Viv and Cyril aren't crazy about all the upheaval, but they'll like the new place. It has a big yard."

"I could tell from the pictures."

The waitress arrives to take their orders and returns with coffee. Lucy adds cream and sugar to hers and takes a sip. "How about you? Anything new?"

John, who has picked up his coffee but not tasted it, carefully sets the cup down.

"Actually, there is something I want to tell you."

Lucy experiences a moment of alarm. Could he have received some bad news about his health? He is her age, fifty-six, but his father only lived to be sixty . . .

"It's sort of hard to know how to say this. To you, I mean." He reaches for her hand. "Lucy, Clare and I . . ."

All at once, Lucy knows what it must be. Not illness or death—life. He is about to tell her that he and Clare are having a baby.

Old habit takes over—she finds herself trying to make it easier for him.

"I suppose that you . . . I mean, it would be natural . . . You and I used to plan . . ."

Years back, when they both went for fertility testing, the specialists told Lucy that her chances of becoming pregnant were near zero. John's prospects for fatherhood were not much better, but of course there have been advances . . . .

She sees that John is about to speak, and lets him. He puts his other hand over the one that is holding hers.

"We're getting a divorce," he says.

The surprise of what she has just heard does nothing to restore Lucy's power of speech. Her mind is searching for the right response to the news that her ex is about to become somebody else's ex.

I'm sorry to hear that.

Well, that's a surprise. (No. Sounds sarcastic.)

Good for you. (Jesus, no.)

"What happened?" she asks, and immediately wonders if the question is overly intrusive. Lucy has never liked inquisitive people.

But John shrugs, apparently taking no offence. "Nothing in particular. Mostly it's the age thing." He gives Lucy the grin she knows so well—it is surprisingly boyish still. "She says the Beatles and the Monkees sound the same."

This is sacrilege indeed. In the sixties, John spent hours trying to imitate McCartney's warble on *Yesterday*. He wore a groove in the *Revolver* album so that the needle would always skip at the beginning of *Eleanor Rigby*.

Lucy is full of questions but holds off asking them, knowing this unexpected news has not really sunk in. Just then, the food arrives. The waitress sets everything down, pours more coffee, and asks, "Will there be anything else?"

"Yes," Lucy says, and points. "Could he have some extra mayonnaise?"

In the weeks that follow, John's announcement comes back to Lucy at odd times. Sometimes because in packing she has come across a photo, a tape, her copy of the *Peterson Field Guide to Birds*, inscribed *For my bird. Christmas, 1980. Love, John.* But at times without any apparent association her mind dwells on the fact that John will be—free?—again. Once, such a turn of events would have meant everything to her.

Viv, the more high strung of the two dogs, develops an eye infection that for all Lucy knows could be psychosomatic. A moving company representative is on his way to give Lucy an estimate, so she calls John to ask him to take Viv to the vet. He readily agrees, coming by in half an hour to collect the dog. Lucy can hear both dogs scrabbling and yipping in the front hall, and John's voice saying, "Poor puppy! Is my Viv under the weather?"

The moving company guy arrives as John is getting Viv into his truck—no easy task. Lucy sees him stop to talk to John, and feels a familiar exasperation. Just like a man to assume that the first man he sees must be in charge. But then Lucy sees the mover pet Viv's head. Maybe he just likes dogs.

She accompanies the mover through the house as he makes notes on a clipboard, pointing to items and asking if they will be going. The appliances, no. The books, yes. A homemade bookcase from college days, no. Dog beds, sea chest, footstool, steel wastebasket, yes.

John returns with pills and ointment for Viv, brushing aside Lucy's offer to write him a check. "It would be no problem for me to stop by on my way to work and give her these," he says, handing over the medications.

"No, thanks," Lucy says, and adds, "I've been giving them pills for quite a while."

John seems unfazed by any implication that she has been the one to deal, every day, with the needs of aging pets. "I'm off then. If you need anything else . . . ." He is jiggling the door latch in the way that will keep it from sticking. "Lucy?"

"Hmmm?"

"I just wanted you to know that I've moved out."

"Oh." Once again, she is at a loss for a response. She takes hold of Viv's collar to prevent the dog from following John out the door.

"That's a big step," is all she can finally come up with.

Between the estimate and her actual moving date, Lucy has three weeks. At times she is overwhelmed by the fact that every single thing has to be out of the house for the buyer's walk through next month. But John is a big help. He takes unwanted items to the dump, walks the dogs, even renails the loose back of a Shaker dresser he made for Lucy from a kit. On the days she's out of lunch provisions, he drives to McDonald's and brings back food which they eat out of the wrappers, as if they were still in college. He doesn't mention Clare, and Lucy doesn't ask.

On the Friday before Lucy's weekend move, she tells John she wants to buy him dinner. "You've been terrific, my friend. Let me take you somewhere with tablecloths while I still have one decent outfit that's not in a box."

John looks at her intently. "Do you think we could have something here? Not for you to cook—I don't mean that. But maybe pizza. The dogs would like that." He scratches Cyril's head, which is resting on John's shoe.

"You're a cheap date, I must say."

"We aim to please. Hey, Luce—remember that place where no matter how many times you said no anchovies they put them on anyway?"

"Notis Pizza. Their slogan was You'll Notis the Difference. Which wasn't necessarily a good thing."

Lucy rummages in the unsealed box that holds paper plates and plastic utensils and a few other items she and the dogs might need when they arrive in Maine. John sees candles in the box and insists on lighting them, even though they're squat white ones intended for power outages. Viv puts her long nose close to the flame, and Lucy calls to her.

"You, there—Viv. Get away from that. We don't need you back at the vet with a singed nose."

They sit on the floor with their backs to the cluttered sofa, feeding bits of cheese and sausage to the dogs, who take the food carefully, as they have been taught. Gathering up the napkins and used forks, Lucy says, "Take what's left, O.K.? My refrigerator's defrosted."

"What will you have for breakfast?"

"I've got some of those chocolate chip bars. And these guys have their dry food."

John gets up slowly, steadying himself against the sofa. When Lucy first knew him, she loved the way he could rise from a cross-legged position in one fluid motion. She can almost see that boy, superimposed on this gray-haired man who has had two disk surgeries.

"Well, I guess I should get going. What time is the truck coming?"

"They said eight."

"Are you sure you don't need me to keep the dogs while they're loading everything?"

"No—but thanks. It's easier this way. They'll just stay in the crate until it's ready to go in my car."

"Okay. So long, you guys. Don't go chasing after any bears."

Lucy realizes that he is stalling. "John," she says. He looks up from giving the dogs one more scratch. "I just want to say . . . about you and Clare . . . I hope that, well, it works out . . ."

"Works out." It is not a question. What is this strange tone?

"I mean, that what you want works out. Whatever will make you happy . . ."

He straightens up and draws in a breath. Now or never, the inhalation seems to say.

"Lucy, I haven't been happy since you and I broke up."

Lucy stares at him. Perhaps she should have seen this coming—the relaxed intimacy of the past month, the constant references to a shared past—but she had so much going on . . .

With the words out, John begins to speak rapidly.

"We could do it. Remember all the times we talked about moving to Maine someday? It was never you going by yourself. Lucy—" he seems to catch her disbelieving expression—"I know you must think I've lost my mind. Or that this has something to do with Clare, but it doesn't. I'm splitting with her because I want you to see how serious I am about us getting back together."

The last phrase hangs in the air. What she would once have given to hear those words.

Viv is watching them both with an anxious expression. From a puppy, she was always able to pick up on tension. Lucy reaches to pet her, then lets her hand drop.

"John, I don't know what to say."

"Of course you don't! I know this must be coming out of the blue for you. But it's been on my mind ever since you told me you were moving. Just say you'll think about it."

"John . . ."

"Once you're settled in, I could drive up. We could have dinner at the inn. You'd have had time to think this over. It wouldn't be so sudden . . . ."

78

"John, I can't."

His flow of eager words stops as abruptly as it began. Pain floods his eyes. Lucy closes her own eyes—she has never been able to bear seeing him hurt. And this time, she knows she has the power to take away the hurt.

"Is there someone else?" he says stiffly.

"No, of course not." She tries to make a small joke. "If there were, I'd say he's been pretty useless in the last month or so."

"That's what I mean! You and me, things like they used to be . . ."

"I'm sorry, but it's too late for things to be that way."

"It's not!"

Lucy knows she must put an end to this. "Johnny, it is. We aren't getting back together. Ever."

She sees two emotions flash across his face. First, hope—at hearing the old nickname. Then despair. Lucy knows she can't let him speak before she's finished.

"John," she says, deliberately rescinding the nickname, "do you remember that time the Coles went on a cruise?" The unhip Coles had been friends of John's parents.

"What possible connection does that have to us?"

"We had to look at all those slides . . . ." She suddenly remembers how she and John had giggled in bed afterwards, making fun of the endless boring shots of the ocean or people holding drinks, and has to swallow before continuing. "They told us about crossing the international dateline."

"I still don't see . . ."

"They thought they had to tell us that it doesn't really exist. As if we were going to think there was a line in the middle of the ocean. But they said that when the ship passes that spot everybody cheers, and they have champagne."

In her mind's eye she can see it. The great ship all lit up, the stars overhead, festive crowds on the deck. The non-existent line approached, then crossed. A day lost or gained, with nowhere to go but forward.

"John," Lucy says gently. "We've crossed that line."

They don't talk as he gathers up his things to leave. Lucy should be relieved to see that he has given up, but the slump of his shoulders and the beaten expression on his face fill her with sadness. When he leans down automatically to give Cyril a last ear tug, he looks every bit his age.

"Will you call me in the morning?" he asks, very formal, as if he were a neighbor who has stopped by.

"Of course. And I'll call you with my number as soon as the phone's in. We'll be fine."

She regrets her choice of pronoun for a moment, but he seems to understand that "we" means Lucy and the dogs.

"I'll wait to hear from you." He kisses her quickly, not meeting her eyes, and lets himself out. In a minute, she hears his truck start.

Lucy stands in the silent house. She knows that she is not yet feeling what has just happened. She looks at the spot where they had their college dorm meal, and thinks she shouldn't have given the dogs pizza. It will be her own fault if they're sick in the car tomorrow.

A tune comes into Lucy's head. Not the Beatles, but early Dylan. The one about remembering people you were once so close to, gone now without a trace.

Lucy begins to hum the song. It was John who had the golden voice, but Lucy no longer worries about her limited range or her tendency to go flat in certain keys. The lyrics come to her in bits and pieces, a lament for lost times and lost people. She comes to the last verse, with its futile wish.

"I'd give it all gladly," Lucy sings, and knows she wouldn't.

WINDFALLS

*F*or Lucy and John's first vacation since a two-day honeymoon five years ago, Lucy's friend Meg has found them a desert island.

"Not *literally*," Meg's voice, characteristically sounding the italics, comes over the phone in Lucy's kitchen. "But there's only maybe fifty people there, tops. And the A-frame is way down at the end. You won't believe the view."

Meg comes from money. She and her family spent summers on an island in Maine—not the one Lucy and John are going to. She and Lucy have been friends forever.

"It's *private*. Just you and loverboy and the waves and birds."

Lucy has an unsettling thought. Meg knows, of course she does, that Lucy and John have had somber news about their chances for conceiving a baby. But the doctor did tell them to relax and maybe consider getting away for a bit. Can Meg be thinking in that impulsive head of hers that a desert island might be just the place for the unlikely to happen?

Lucy promises postcards—"If you have time," Meg says, further strengthening Lucy's suspicions. They hang up, and Lucy stands for a moment with her hand on the phone, wondering whether this trip is really such a good idea.

The two hour boat ride to the island is a rough one—choppy waves, drifting fog, a cold spray that makes Lucy glad of her new warm jacket. She and John sit on a damp bench in the stern, holding hands. He gives her hand an excited squeeze as the island finally appears, very close. Lucy sees a cluster of houses, their paint peeled away by the salt air, and a dock that the captain is steering toward. The boat bumps, the captain throws the tie line to someone on the dock, and the passengers stand, a little unsteadily.

A small crowd is waiting as the passengers climb the iron ladder and step onto the wharf. One of these sunburned natives must be Henry Morgan, whose wife Lucy has been corresponding with. She sees a man with red hair approaching John.

"John? Henry Morgan."

The two men shake hands, and John waves Lucy over for introductions. Lucy likes Henry Morgan's low, rich voice, every word distinct. Later she will learn he has been an actor and a drama coach.

"That's all you've got?" Henry asks when Lucy points out their luggage—two sleeping bags and two cardboard boxes. Lucy feels an odd sense of pride—she and John are not like those stick in the muds who bring their whole house with them when they travel.

Henry stows the boxes and bags in the rear of his ancient Volvo. It appears to have once been light blue, but now looks as if rust is all that's holding it together. A crooked bumper sports a sticker reading Life Is Too Short To Drink Bad Wine. One rear door is tied with string, and the back windshield is a plastic bag.

"I'll sit back here," Lucy says, opening the door that still has a handle. John gets in front next to Henry, who declaims, "Squaws in back!" and starts the car with a noise like small arms fire.

The dirt road that curves up from the harbor intersects with a slightly wider road running north and south. The sky is a deeper blue than Lucy can ever remember seeing. She and John gaze out at houses, piled lobster traps, a small graveyard, as Henry describes in colorful detail who lives in each of the places they are passing.

His own house has flowers and tomato plants in front—right after it, Henry turns down a rutted path lined with blackberry vines.

"Vehicles are verboten on this road," he says. "It'll be nice and quiet for you."

He pulls to a stop in front of a shingled A-frame with huge front windows facing the ocean. Meg was right—the view is breathtaking. A grassy meadow sloping down to the water, sparkling with light, small islands rising from it.

"I'll just show you a couple of things," Henry says, "then I'll leave you to get settled. Just walk up to the house if you need anything."

Lucy tries to pay attention. How to light the stove. How often to check the gauge on the propane tank. Where the lobster picks and nutcrackers are kept. Henry is bringing lobsters back from the harbor when he goes to collect his mail. Lucy's attention keeps returning to the flawless September day framed by the big windows.

Henry drives off in his wake-the-dead Volvo and John and Lucy climb the steep ladder to the second floor, carrying the sleeping bags. Fresh, cool air blows through from the open windows at either end. As she is spreading one of the bags on the double bed, Lucy feels John's hands encircle her waist from behind. She turns, and he grins at her and pulls off his T-shirt. Lucy returns the grin and begins unbuttoning her own shirt.

An hour later, dozing on top of the sleeping bag, the second one covering them, they are awakened by a voice that sounds very close.

"Lobsters." It is Henry at the back door. John and Lucy look at each other wildly, trying not to giggle.

"Coming," John calls down. He throws aside the sleeping bag and picks up his jeans. Lucy watches as he puts them on, ducks his head under the low doorway, and climbs shirtless and shoeless down the ladder. While the two men talk, Lucy dresses, then goes to the window to watch Henry pull away.

"He was smiling," she tells John as she joins him downstairs. "I mean *really* smiling. I think he knew what we'd been doing."

"Oh, well—he probably does it himself now and then." John looks doubtful, though—Henry must be in his fifties.

Their days on the island take on a rhythm. Morning coffee on the deck, long walks, the beach at midday with a picnic lunch. Evenings after dinner, they walk past the Morgans' house and follow a path that loops along the cliffs above the ocean and circles back to where it began. In the darkness, they find the house by the one light left burning. "In the spirit of thrift," John had said, on their first night in the house. On a day of pouring rain they sit on the floor putting together a jigsaw puzzle of state flags. There isn't a chance it has all its pieces.

One glittering afternoon they are reading on the musty tan quilt which Henry's wife Gwen has said is for the beach. Around them, seagulls are warring for the remains of their tuna sandwiches. John suddenly sits up, shading his eyes.

"Luce—will you look at that."

She raises herself onto her elbows and looks where he is pointing. On the horizon, moving toward the beach, is a toy-like yellow kayak. John and Lucy watch as the kayaker turns the boat to let the waves carry it onto the sand.

"I'd love to get one of those," John says. "Imagine being out there, away from everything. It must be incredible."

A dozen objections crowd Lucy's mind. Where would he learn to use it? What if it capsized? She is pretty sure there are no sharks in Maine, but what if a seal came up under the boat . . .

She looks at John's face. He is fair-skinned, but the glow she sees is not from the sun.

"What color?" she says.

* * *

The eve of departure. Everything is packed, the dishes washed and on the drain board, a fire burning in the woodstove. Lucy and John lie together on the sofa, a sagging yellow relic brought to within inches of the floor by their weight.

"They can't make us leave, can they?" John asks reasonably.

"What could they do," Lucy responds, "if we just said we weren't going."

"We could catch fish, and pick berries."

"And burn driftwood in the stove."

They lie pressed together, his arms around her, everything quiet except the snapping of birch logs in the stove. Both of them drift off to sleep, awakening in a cold room that smells of ashes.

There is just time for a last morning walk the length of the island. The blackberries are ripe, and a few windy nights have brought down small, bumpy apples, mottled yellow and red. Lucy stoops with the ease of youth to gather a handful.

"Fifty years from now," she says, "we'll be coming here with . . ."

"Our walkers?"

She gives silent thanks for John's levity. She had almost said *with our grandchildren*.

"Right. And our matching baggy sweaters. And we'll be tottering around picking up these . . ."

Lucy opens her hand and holds out to him the bright, sweet-smelling fruit, a season's windfalls.